JENNA AND THE LEGEND

OF THE WHITE WOLF
THE ITURIA CHRONICLES

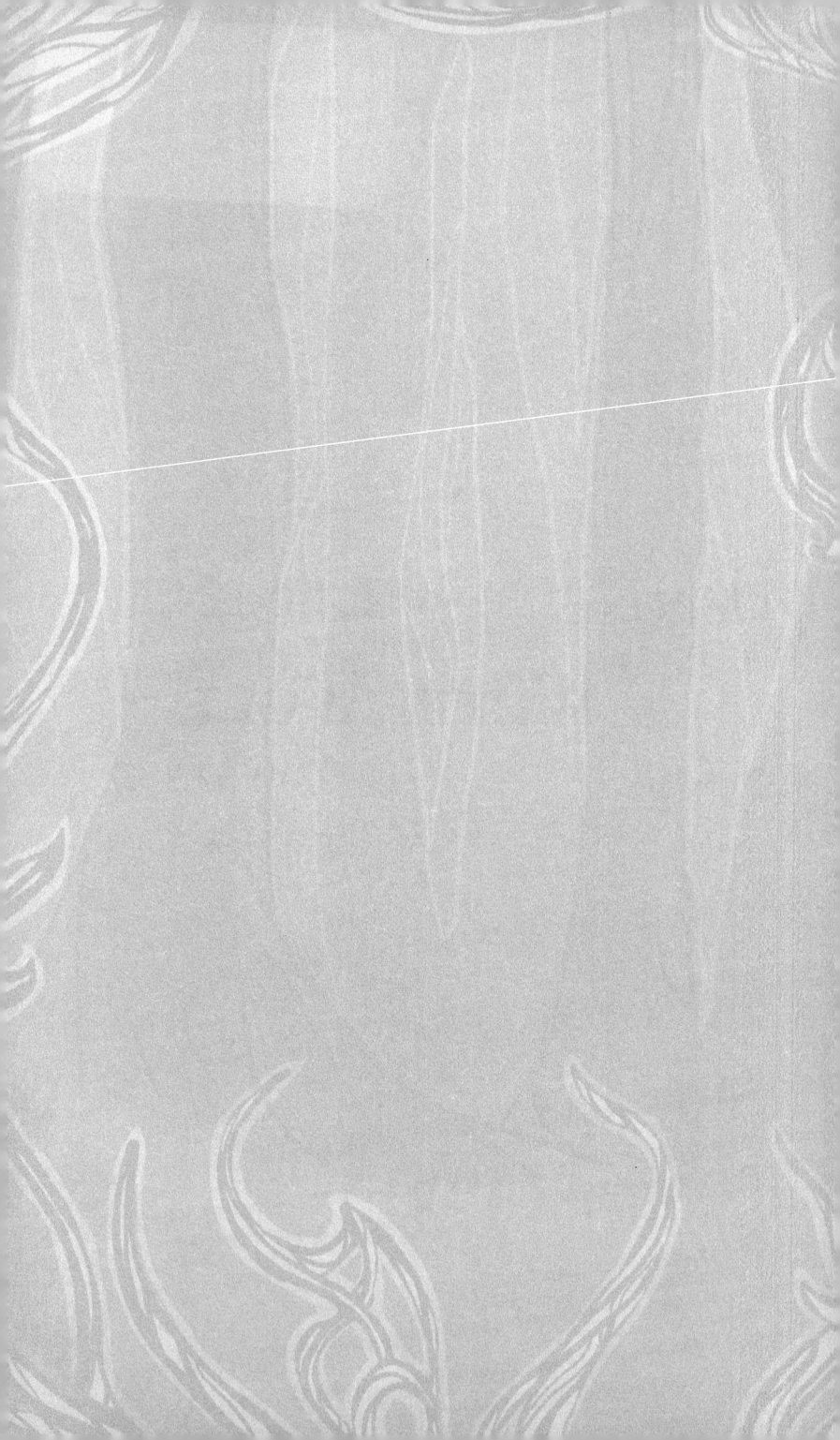

BOOK 3

JENNA AND THE LEGEND OF THE WHITE WOLF
THE ITURIA CHRONICLES

J.B. Moonstar

The Little
Horsemen™

Published By: The Little Horsemen an imprint of 4 Horsemen Publications, Inc.

The Little Horsemen Publications
℅ 4 Horsemen Publications, Inc.
PO Box 419
Sylva, NC 28779
4horsemenpublications.com
info@4horsemenpublications.com

Cover & Illustration by Jenn Kotick. Contact for commssions at Jkotickart@gmail.com .
Typesetting by Michelle Cline

Library of Congress Control Number: 2021936527

Paperback ISBN: 978-1-64450-223-5
Ebook ISBN: 978-1-64450-222-8
Audio ISBN: 978-1-64450-221-1
Hardcover ISBN: 978-1-64450-649-3

DEDICATION

Th is book is dedicated to my wonderful and talented daughter, Jennifer, with thanks for all her love, support, and encouragement, and for her help in bringing Ituria's world to life!

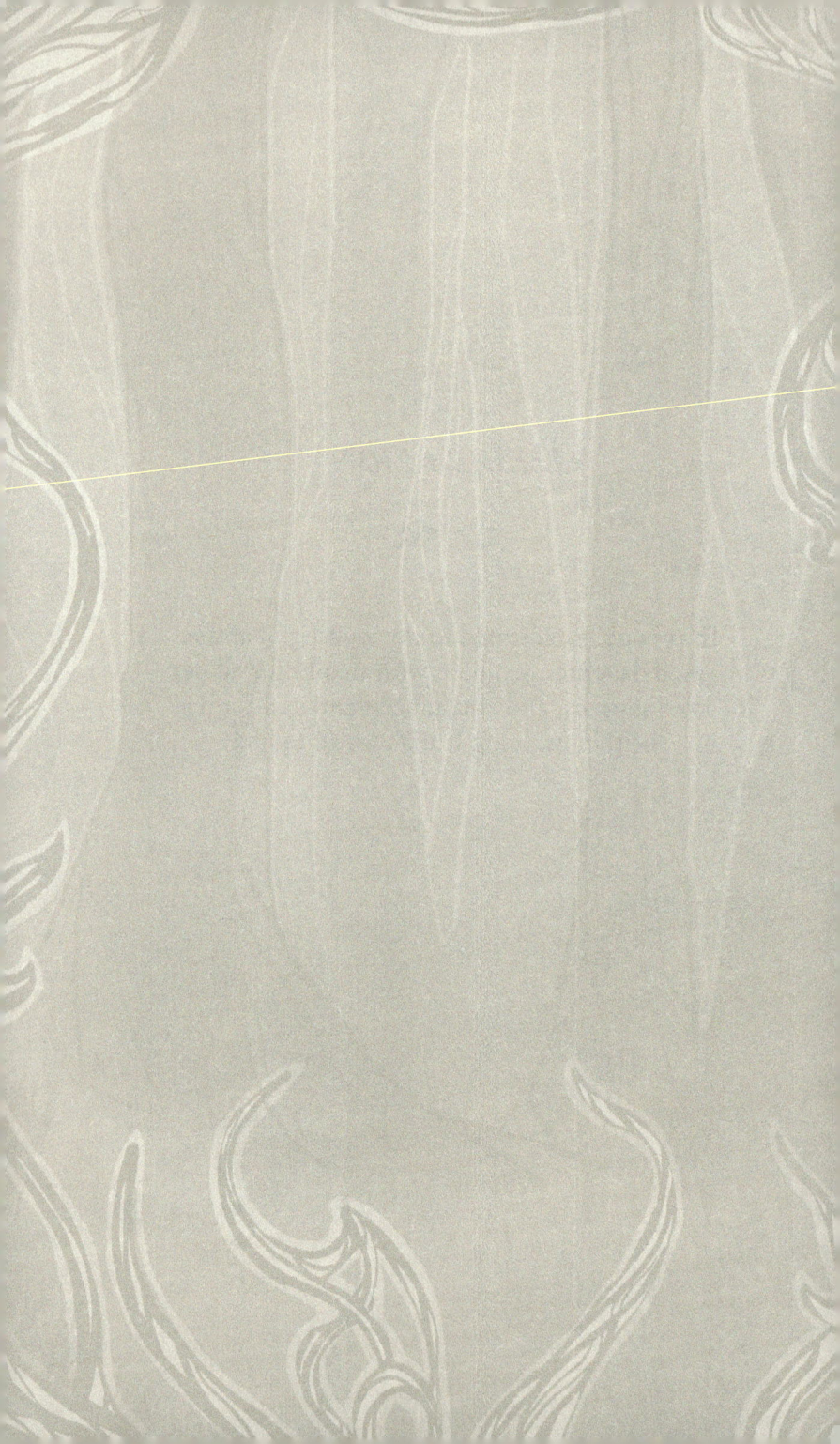

Dear Reader,

In my continuing compilation of the interactions between Ituria's realm and the human world, this story takes place as Ituria is trying to resolve a territory border issue between competing wolf packs on Earth.

While on this mission, Ituria was trapped by human hunters, and the magic of his Earth-forest home transforms Jenna into a wolf to help free him. Jenna and her new forest friends must first rescue Ituria and then trick the hunters into leaving the forest.

During her quest, Jenna learns how she fits into the Legend of the White Wolf and must decide if she is brave enough to see it through!

Sincerely,

Knocker,

First Guard to Ituria

Table of Contents

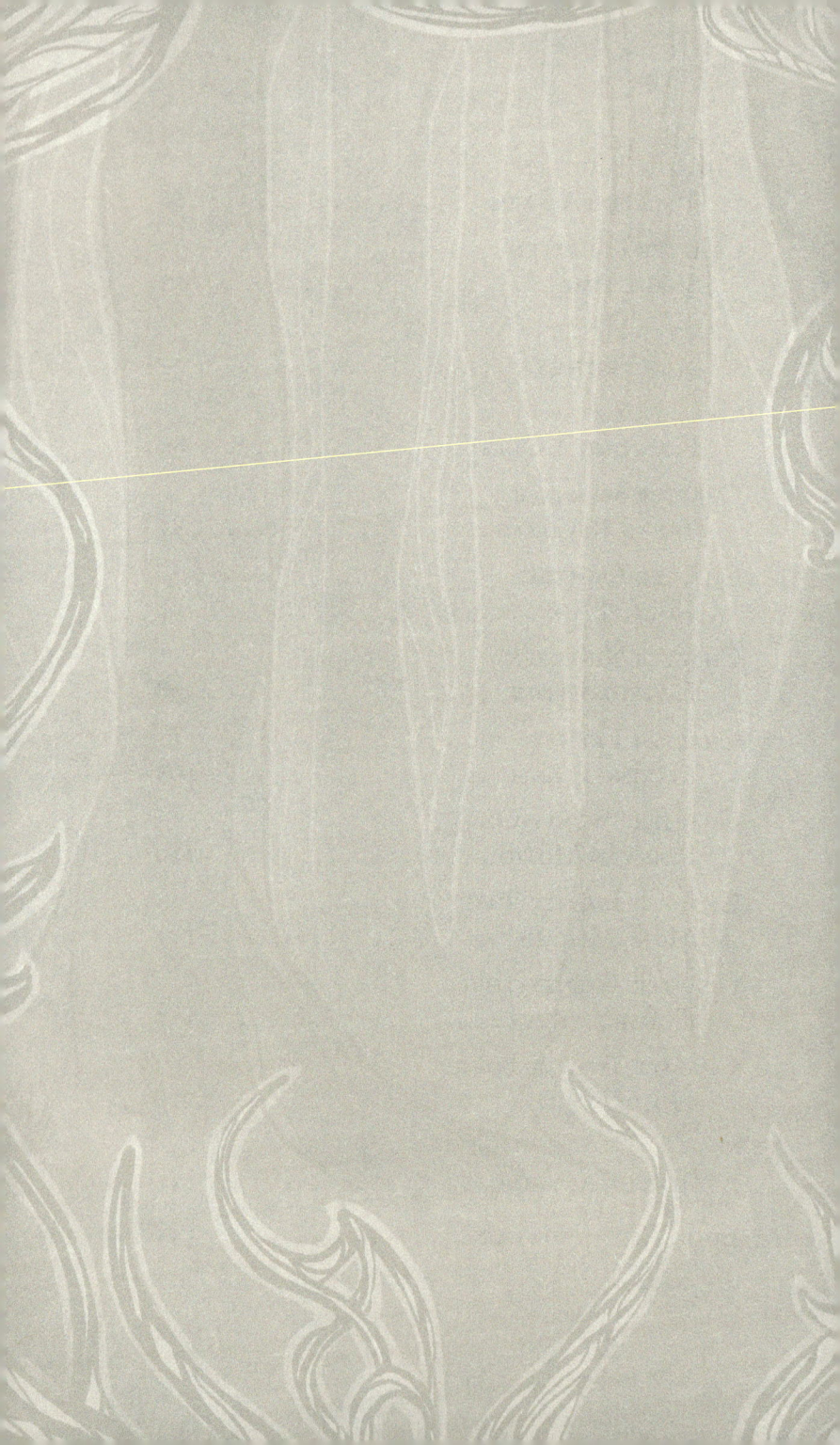

Chapter One

TRANSFORMATION

"Jenna, get in here and clean your room!" her sister yelled.

Jenna pretended not to hear and kept her head buried in her book. Being a military family, they moved a lot. Just before her dad was deployed a few months ago, the family moved into another new house; this one backed up to a large forest.

Before her dad left, he told her older sister, Sandy, to help mom take care of things, which Sandy took to heart, bossing Jenna around at every opportunity as soon as mom would head off to work. Jenna escaped the constant nagging by sitting in the back yard reading, and sometimes she caught glimpses of the wild creatures in the woods behind her house. These became her imaginary friends, her only friends in this new house. She liked to talk to them, imagining they understood and could talk back to her.

A high-pitched screech caught her attention as it almost drowned out her sister calling her yet again. Looking in the direction it came from, she saw a large hawk perched in a pine tree at the far edge of her back yard. She followed its gaze to see a squirrel crouched in the grass.

"Uh oh," she said quietly to herself, still watching the squirrel.

Suddenly, the squirrel jumped up and ran in her direction, only to get about halfway to her and then turn and dash quickly back into a nearby tree. It started chattering loudly, waving its tail, its shiny black eyes looking directly at her.

Worried the loud noise and movements of the squirrel would draw the hawk's attention, Jenna turned to look at the hawk. Surprisingly, it was looking back at her. The squirrel had stopped chattering and she turned to see it was again slowly, inch by inch, creeping toward her.

Staying as still as possible, she looked back and forth between the squirrel and hawk, waiting to see what would happen. *What did the squirrel want from her?* It made several more attempts to reach Jenna, making it only halfway, then scampering back to the tree.

Then something else caught Jenna's eye. Just coming out of the forest was a fox, cautiously walking toward her, its black eyes focused on her.

Within a few feet of Jenna, it stopped, sat down, and barked at her quickly for a few seconds, staring straight into Jenna's dark brown eyes. Jenna stared back, not knowing how to react, was it hungry? Was it looking for a place to sleep? And why were all the animals acting so strangely today?

The fox barked twice quickly, slowly lifted its white paw to about its shoulder level and reached it out toward Jenna. *What did it want her to do?* It must be trying to tell her something, she just didn't understand what.

Not getting a reaction from Jenna, the fox turned its head to look at its raised paw, it looked directly at her, back at its paw, and back at her. This fox acted like it wanted her to touch its paw. *But why?* It didn't seem to want to hurt her. Maybe it just needed a friend, she could relate to that. Slowly, she raised her arm and put her hand on the fox's paw.

The instant she touched its paw, a giant wave of dizziness struck her, knocking her back into her chair, dazed and confused. She closed her eyes and shook her head a few times to try and clear her mind. After a few seconds, she opened her eyes to see what happened to the fox, and she saw it running back into the forest. She tried to get up and run after it, but she couldn't stand up, and she tumbled forward onto the ground. *What was happening?*

Looking down at her feet, they were covered in white fur, her hands had become paws; her whole body had become that of a wolf—she was covered in thick white fur from head to toe! Looking quickly back at the fox, it had stopped to see why she wasn't following him. The fox didn't seem to notice the dramatic change in Jenna's appearance, and called to her, "Come on, we haven't much time!"

Jenna tried to figure out this transformation, and then realized the fox was talking to her in growls and barks—and she understood him! The fox exclaimed urgently, "We must hurry, before it's too late!"

His voice sounded so worried and anxious that Jenna felt compelled to help her new animal friend, despite her drastic change in appearance. She got up and tried to stand on her new wolf legs. A little shaky at first, her balance soon returned, and she followed him into the woods. Within a few minutes, running as a wolf seemed so natural, she had no problem keeping up.

The fox said no more until they came to a clearing in the forest. Among the ferns and flowers, there were two squirrels and two small deer talking to each other. As she entered the clearing, they immediately stopped talking and turned as one, staring at Jenna. The deer were visibly frightened by the white wolf, shaking and huddling together, but the fox was quick to say, "Don't worry, this is Jenna, she has come to help us save Ituria!"

The fox turned back to Jenna. "I am Ralphie, one of the animals who live in this forest. Ituria is trapped and we only have a short time before Ranco finds him, so we must hurry!"

Jenna didn't know who Ituria or Ranco were, and she had questions, lots of questions. Trying to respond, she found herself growling and barking, but she understood the wolf talk, and so did the animals in the clearing. She could talk with the animals!

"Wait a second," she barked. "Who is Ituria and why do we need to rescue him?"

Chapter Two

THE SEARCH FOR ITURIA

"Ituria," Ralphie answered, "is the leader and protector of our forest. He has been caught in a hunter's net, and we must get to him before Ranco does or Ranco will kill him. Ranco is a grey wolf from the North Forest who has invaded our home and has been killing the residents."

A squirrel quickly jumped onto a stump and started speaking in squirrel, with squeaks and clicks, now easily understood by Jenna. "I'm Sedric," he said. "I saw Ituria trapped in the net and tried to talk to you earlier this evening, but you were human and so big, you scared me, so I ran away. Now you are much more beautiful in your wolfskin, and I see that you can help us. Legend has it a white wolf will come to help our leader when he is in need. We've seen you come to the edge of the forest and talk and sing to us, and sometimes the image of a white wolf would cover your human body. That's how we knew you were the one to find!"

Jenna was amazed. She had seen the animals in the forest numerous times and talked to them, pretending they would answer. When she was lonely, she would sing to the trees and grass, imagining she helped them grow. Now she was in the forest in the form of a powerful white wolf, and she was talking to these animals, and they understood her!

Ralphie interrupted her thoughts with his urgent request, "Enough idle chatter! We must hurry or we will be too late!" Ralphie headed away from the group, looking back and calling, "Sedric, you know where to go, so you must show us."

Without a moment's hesitation, Jenna knew she must help these small, brave animals, or they would not be able to save their leader. Her dad always told her it was the duty of the strong to help those in need. These small animals needed someone larger and stronger to help them, as they would be no match for an invading wolf. Quite large as a wolf, Jenna suggested, "Sedric, why don't you and the other squirrel ride on my back, then you can direct me, and we can get there quicker."

Nodding in agreement and waving to Fira, he called. "Come on Fira!" Once on Jenna's back, he called to the deer, "Evan and Frieda, you follow close, so we don't lose you, okay?"

The two deer nodded hesitantly and moved a little closer to Jenna. Up until now, they had stayed near the edge of the clearing, cautiously listening.

The group set off at once after Ralphie, Sedric and Fira on Jenna's back, the two young deer following. There was not much of a path, so they had to weave around the thick tree trunks and underbrush.

The sun had set, so only the faint light of dusk lit their way. Soon it would be dark.

They ran through the forest for several minutes when they came to a small clearing with a stream. Once they crossed the stream, Ralphie stopped the group and sniffed—his tail twitching nervously. He said, "The grey wolf has been here. He is ahead of us. We must hurry!"

Moving even faster, Sedric directed the way from Jenna's back. Continuing through the forest for a few more minutes, Jenna smelled something burning and glanced at the fox near her side.

"Smoke from the humans' campfire! We must pass around it quickly and quietly," whispered Ralphie.

They silently passed the camp and continued to the spot where Sedric had seen Ituria, only Ituria was not there!

Ralphie shouted to Sedric, "What happened, where has he gone? Could he have gotten out by himself?"

Sedric shook his head. "No, it was too tight, too much net, he would never have gotten out by himself. I don't see any signs of fighting or blood, so I don't think Ranco got him. What could have happened?"

"What about the camp we passed?" Jenna said with a deep growl. "Let's go look to see if they were hunting and caught him."

Ralphie nodded in agreement. It would be better for the humans to catch Ituria than for the grey wolf to get him, so they circled back to the camp.

Looking through the bushes at the edge of the camp, Jenna and the others saw a large metal cage set back from the fire, barely visible in the dark.

Creeping around the camp and over to the cage, they looked inside. In the shadows of the flickering fire, she saw Ituria for the first time. He was a majestic white unicorn with a long golden horn on his forehead. *Wait, a unicorn?* She had to look again, to make sure she was seeing clearly.

Even trapped, she had never seen anything so magnificent. He was in a cage that was not big enough to hold him standing, so his head was lowered and resting against the hard metal bars of the cage. His eyes were closed. This was so wrong! She had to help save him from the hunters and Ranco, but how?

Even though Jenna had the body of a wolf, she still had the mind and memory of a human. She could see there was a lock on the door of the cage. Somewhere was a key to the lock, and if they could find it, they could use it to free Ituria.

She looked at the hunters gathered around the fire in sleeping bags, and all were asleep. There was one who looked a little older than the rest; he was likely the leader. If so, he would have the key.

Softly she said to Sedric, "Go sneak over by the human on the right. Check his pockets for any small pieces of metal that look like a stick. Be careful not to wake him."

They all watched anxiously as Sedric nimbly jumped over to the hunter.

The man was laying on his side, and there was something in his front shirt pocket. Sedric tried to pull it out, but the hunter turned over, causing Sedric to scramble backward.

Jenna whispered, "Gently now, tickle him on his hand to try and get him to turn over again!"

Sedric cautiously went back and used his tiny paws to touch the man's hand, his little nails touching the open palm. The hunter made a small grunting sound and rolled back over so the pocket was again visible. Sedric started to work again, slowly wiggling out the small object from the pocket.

He had it! A small stick-like metal object Jenna knew was a key. She hoped it was the one that would open the cage. Quietly they went around the outside of camp to the door of the cage.

Ituria had opened his eyes and appeared more alert but didn't speak. He looked exhausted, his head and body leaning on the side of the cage. Jenna was concerned for him and wondered if he would be able to get away once they opened the cage.

Jenna tried to hold the key, but her wolf paw would not allow her to pick it up.

"Ralphie," she said softly, "you must try to open the cage. You take the pointed side of the key and put it in the lock. Then you turn it until you feel it click. We must be quiet!"

Ralphie nodded. However, he could not pick up the key either. They decided Sedric would have to stand on Jenna's back while he tried to open the lock, as Sedric's paws would allow him to grip the key.

Jenna softly called to the two young deer, "You must watch the humans carefully while we free Ituria. If they start to move, let us know."

The deer nodded their heads and turned toward the hunters. Within a few seconds, they backed into Jenna, shaking with fear. Evan backed up even farther until he was next to Jenna's ear, and with a trembling voice, he whispered, "We must hurry. Ranco has found us!"

Chapter Three

THE RESCUE

Turning around to view the camp, Jenna could see the hunters were still sleeping. Then she saw a large grey wolf, barely distinguishable from the shadows; his glowing eyes were reflecting the firelight and watching closely everything they were doing.

They would have to plan this carefully as they could not wake up the hunters. Ranco must know this as well, as the hunters had guns and could kill them all.

Jenna looked back at Ituria; he had lifted his head as best he could in the cramped cage and was trying to appear strong and brave. But she could see in his eyes that he might not be able to outrun the grey wolf in his current condition. What could they do?

Suddenly, something flew down and landed on Jenna's back—it looked like the large hawk she had seen earlier. Without making a sound, it looked intently into Jenna's eyes and Jenna knew it did not want to speak for fear of waking up the hunters. She felt it was telling her it would help any way it could, and she nodded her head, glad for the assistance.

She whispered to the others, "Let's get Ituria free, and then we will have to protect him against Ranco and the hunters. Be prepared to run when we get the cage open. Sedric, is there anywhere safe around here we can take Ituria so we can protect him?"

Sedric nodded, "There's a small cave not too far away, near the stream. It's not big, but it will hold all of us. It's just past the large oak to the north of camp."

"Does everyone know which cave Sedric is talking about?" Jenna asked quietly in low wolf growls. Since Sedric and his friends played together often, they all knew and nodded.

"Ituria, you will go first with Fira," Jenna whispered looking at Ituria, and he nodded to confirm he understood. Turning to Ralphie, she continued, "Ralphie, you and the deer next, follow Ituria. Sedric and I will bring up the back, so I can keep Ranco away if necessary."

Everyone nodded in agreement. Jenna didn't know how she would keep Ranco back, but at least Ituria, who was unable to fight now, would be safe. The hawk landed on Jenna's shoulder, nodded its head once and then flew to a nearby branch; Jenna felt better knowing the hawk would stay nearby to help her.

The plan was set. Sedric quickly jumped up on Jenna's back and put the metal key into the lock. It took a few moments, and with Fira's help, he was able to turn the key enough to unlock the lock. It made a clunking sound as it unlocked, and everyone turned to look at the hunters nervously. One twitched a little, but no one woke.

However, Ranco perked his ears up and was watching them closely. From his crouched position, he slowly started crawling toward the group at the cage, also being careful not to wake the hunters.

"Quickly everyone!" Jenna whispered, "on with the plan. Fira, go to Ituria, I will try and open the cage."

Fira went through the cage bars and got onto Ituria's back. Ituria still had not said anything, and Jenna believed he was saving his strength for the run to the cave. Using her teeth to take the lock off the cage door, she then slowly started to open the door.

A loud creaking sound made her stop instantly. This noise would wake up the hunters. Jenna thought for a moment and realized she could use this to her advantage.

"Listen," she whispered, "when Ranco gets close to the hunters, I will open the cage. It will wake the hunters, and hopefully they will chase him rather than us." Jenna turned to watch Ranco. "Ranco is almost close enough. Ready—now!"

Jenna pulled on the cage door, hard—it opened and made a loud screeching sound, causing the hunters to wake up. Looking around to see what woken them up, they saw Ranco crouching right in the middle of their camp!

Jenna barked, "Run!" She hoped the hunters would be so distracted by Ranco that they would not hear. Ituria, Fira, and the others took off toward the cave.

With Sedric on her back, Jenna started running too, taking a quick glance back and seeing Ranco growling fiercely at the hunters as he backed into the forest on the other side of the camp.

He caught Jenna's eyes as he turned to run away, and his eyes glared at hers—he was furious. Jenna knew at that moment she had made an enemy. The hunters grabbed their guns and nets and ran after him; not yet realizing the cage door had been opened and their prize had escaped.

Jenna disappeared into the shadows with Sedric, hoping the hunters would not follow. Shortly they caught up with Ituria and the others and ran for a few minutes to get to their destination. Jenna saw Ituria was not running fast and seemed to be favoring his right back leg.

Finally, they made it to a cave next to the stream, almost hidden by thick bushes. Ralphie pushed back the bushes so Ituria and Jenna could fit into the cave. It was small, but it looked safe and was hidden from the outside. They would rest here until they came up with another plan, as now they had both the hunters and Ranco to worry about.

At this time, Ituria spoke. "Jenna, thank you, and thanks to your friends for coming to my rescue. I do not know what would have happened if you had not appeared. But you have made an enemy today— Ranco. He will not forget this. If he gets away from the hunters, he will be back to seek his revenge— against you and me."

Jenna was more concerned about Ituria right now than Ranco. "Are you hurt? It seems your back leg is sore when you walk."

"Yes," said Ituria, "It is. I was running from the hunters when something hit me in the leg; it could have been one of their guns. It does not appear to be a major injury, but it did slow me down enough that they were able to throw nets over me, from which I could not escape. As they were taking me to their camp, I saw Ranco in the shadows." He paused for a moment in thought, and then continued.

"I knew Ranco would take any opportunity to rid the forest of me—however he could. Then he would have control. The hunters are looking for more animals, and Ranco was staying just out of their sights, waiting for his chance against me."

"What can we do to help?" asked Ralphie. The others eagerly gathered around to see what they could do to help Ituria.

"If I can rest a little, and possibly get some water and food, I shall be better soon," he replied.

Sedric, Fira, and the deer left the cave to find some fresh grass, and Ralphie used some large wide leaves to fashion a small basket to get water from the stream.

"Please let me check out your injury," Jenna said, "maybe there is something I can do, too."

Ituria nodded and turned so she could see his back leg. The full moon shining in the cave gave enough light to inspect the leg. It indeed had a wound that looked like a bullet had grazed it, and it had left a gash several inches long. Even though it wasn't bleeding much, it must be painful to move. She didn't know what she could do to make it any better. Was there a way to put a bandage on it, or some healing plants? She agreed with Ituria that he needed to rest, and they would think about plans in the morning.

The other animals came back with some food, and Ituria ate, drank some water, and then suggested everyone try to sleep. It would be a busy morning tomorrow.

Jenna tried to rest, but could not sleep. She walked to the front of the cave and sat facing the entrance. In the distance, she could hear Ranco's howls.

He had escaped the hunters, but was now calling out into the night, "White wolf, I am coming for you—you will not escape me! This is my forest!" Jenna knew she had made a fearsome enemy, and finally fell into a troubled sleep, trying to remember how she got into this situation.

Chapter Four

A Visitor
In The Night

Jenna awoke and realized she was still in a cave, and it was dark. Still in the form of a wolf, her new wolf senses had awakened her, telling her something was wrong.

She walked to the back of the cave, checking on the others. The moonlight allowed her to see where Ituria was still sleeping; all the smaller creatures were gathered around him, sleeping as well.

It was not they who had awakened her. There was something though, but she couldn't figure it out yet. She turned and walked back to the front of the cave.

Peering through the bushes, she could just make out the figure of a wolf in the moonlight, maybe a hundred feet or so from the cave. He wasn't looking her way; he was sniffing the ground, trying to find something. She turned and quietly backed into the cave, hoping he hadn't seen her.

This must be Ranco, thought Jenna, who would have tracked them from the hunters' camp. There was no howling now; this wolf was tracking, not wanting his prey to know where he was. Jenna sat down, trying to think of what to do.

If Ituria was strong, he could help fight off the wolf, but he was weakened and wounded, and she was not sure what he could do if the wolf found them.

She may be a wolf now, but she had never fought another wolf before; she was still a girl inside. Did she have the strength and fierceness to defend her friends? *What would she do if the wolf showed up at the front of the cave?* She did not know.

Ituria seemed to sense Jenna was awake, as he woke too. He asked quietly, "What is wrong, Jenna? Why aren't you sleeping?"

"There is a large wolf outside the cave. He has not found us yet, but he is looking. I am afraid it is Ranco. I heard Ranco earlier crying out he was looking for the white wolf. I don't know how to fight. What can I do if he finds us in the cave?"

"I understand your concerns," said Ituria quietly. "I know you are not from this forest and are not what you appear to be."

Jenna realized Ituria knew she was not really a wolf, so she would not have the experience as a wolf required to fight off another wolf—especially a large wolf like Ranco.

"If Ranco finds us," continued Ituria, "Ranco would not hesitate to kill you and all of the other animals just to get to me." Ituria tried to stand up, but his back leg was stiff, and it was difficult. He may be able to defend them for a while, but since he did not have all his strength or agility, it would be a hard fight.

Looking at Jenna he continued, "I will lead the fight if Ranco comes in. You must protect the little animals and get them to the forest to be safe. Once they are safe, if you are able, you can come back to help me. A wolf is vulnerable from behind. If Ranco is challenging me, you can come up from behind and bite him on the back of his neck. You must bite hard, to break his neck bone."

Ituria could see Jenna's eyes widen as she was contemplating such a vicious attack. He continued, "Or, if you can only get him from the side, you must grab a back leg and bite down hard, trying to break a leg bone. Your jaws as a wolf are strong; you can bite hard enough to crack a bone."

Jenna's human gasp translated into a canine's huff as Ituria continued. "However, do not grab a front leg, as Ranco can turn his head and grab the back of your neck. Ranco will want to kill me first, so may forget you are around—especially if he sees you leaving with the other animals. Do you understand?"

Jenna nodded, and she felt a little better now. At least Ituria understood the situation and had told her how she would have to fight. She did not know if she could, but at least they had a plan. They were both quiet and listened for any sounds.

A little while later, Jenna heard the screech of the hawk and stood up. She walked to the front of the cave and again looked out through the bushes. The wolf was still out there in the shadows, a little closer now. It was not moving; it was sitting by the stream, as if waiting. She still was not sure if it was Ranco or not; the shape was not quite the same, but she didn't get a good look at Ranco at the hunter's camp. If it wasn't him, it might be one of his friends, waiting for him to arrive.

Suddenly, the wolf looked up, looking directly at her through the bushes.

Jenna was scared, *it had found them*, she thought. *It was waiting until they attempted to leave the cave before attacking.*

Jenna quickly looked around to see if there were any other wolves out there by the stream. Would they be ambushed as they came out in the morning?

"Friend of Ituria," called the wolf softly, "I am not your enemy. My name is Trent. I heard Ranco's howling, and I have come to protect you from him. I know you are scared, so I am waiting until morning when you and your group have had a chance to rest. You are safe for now. Go back and sleep; we will talk in the morning."

At this, Jenna heard the hawk's cry again, as if to confirm it was not Ranco.

Jenna felt relieved it was not Ranco, but was still afraid of this new wolf, and of what the morning would bring.

Chapter Five

A MEETING WITH TRENT

Jenna was glad Ranco had not yet found them, but she wasn't sure what to think about the new wolf sitting down by the stream. While Trent said he would watch out for them and she could sleep, she knew she could not. Too much had happened, and there was still so much she didn't understand. She looked over at Ituria, who was awake and looking at her.

"He says his name is Trent, do you know of him?" she asked.

Ituria nodded, "Yes, he is the pack leader of the West Forest wolves. He is a good leader and will help us while we are in Middle Forest."

"What is Middle Forest?" Jenna replied as she walked over and sat down next to Ituria. "I thought the forest was the forest?"

"To humans, yes. But not to the animals who live here." Jenna tilted her head and looked at him with confusion, and he explained. "There are several sections ruled by pack leaders, as the wolf packs are the most powerful animals in this area. Trent is the pack

22

leader of the West Forest; he has been so for several years. Ranco is the pack leader of the North Forest, and he has been trouble since he became leader about a year ago. There used to be a pack in the East Forest many years ago, but the humans took over the East Forest and most of the pack was killed. You actually live in East Forest, even though it is not much of a forest anymore."

"Where are we now—what is Middle Forest?" Jenna was trying to follow the different forests—which to her were previously just "the forest."

"The Middle Forest is my domain, and each animal that enters into it is bound by my law to be peaceful. The animals who live in Middle Forest are safe from being hunted by the other animals. Once outside of Middle Forest, though, the law of nature rules, as wolves, foxes and other meat eaters also have the right to live and eat as nature intended. Your home lays on the boundary of Middle Forest and what was East Forest."

"What is Ranco doing out of the North Forest then?" she asked. "Why is he after you?"

"Ranco does not believe the ruler of each section of the forest can make the rules." Ituria replied, "He believes he should be able to hunt in Middle Forest, along with his North Forest."

Then Ituria's voice got low and sorrowful. "The animals in Middle Forest have lived in peace for so long," he said, shaking his head, "They are not used to being hunted and were easy prey for Ranco and his pack. Since Ranco took control of the North

Forest wolves, many of my friends have been killed. He would kill me, too, if he got the chance."

"What about Trent, does he follow your rules?" Jenna was worried about the wolf outside. What did he think about Ituria's rule of Middle Forest, and what would he think about her—a wolf who did not have a pack?

Ituria looked at Jenna and nodded. "Trent and I have been friends for many years. We understand and respect the rules for each of the Forests we rule, and we have had no problems. Trent has a strong pack, and West Forest is large enough to sustain them well. I do trust him, and you can too."

Jenna was relieved; at least she could trust the wolf outside to protect her and the others. She thought it might be good to talk to Trent about what they needed to do to get Ituria back to his home in Middle Forest. Trent would know what was going on outside of the cave, and they could plan together.

"Do you think I should talk to Trent about what is happening outside?" Jenna asked Ituria. "He might know what is going on and possibly what happened to Ranco."

"That's a good idea," he responded. "We are blocked off in this cave. While being protected, it also keeps us from learning what has happened since we got away from the hunters. Being outside, Trent would be able to hear what is going on, and he may have contacted his pack."

As Jenna got up, Ituria added, "You must not be long, though, as we will have to travel in the morning and you need to get some rest—tomorrow will be a busy day."

"Okay," Jenna agreed, "I will find out what he might know, and see if he can help us get you home."

Jenna walked over to the front of the cave. She peered into the dark forest and could barely make out the shape of Trent next to the stream below. She needed help in getting Ituria back to his home, and Trent would make a good ally. She looked back at Ituria, and then into the darkness.

"Trent," she called quietly, "may we speak?"

"Yes," he said, "come join me by the stream."

Jenna slowly walked down through the bushes to the stream and over to where Trent was sitting.

Even in the dim light of the moon, she could see he was a large wolf and had a powerfully built body. He would make a good friend, and a bad enemy. Still a little cautious, she sat several feet away.

"I told Ituria you are down here, and he says you are the pack leader of the West Forest pack and can be trusted."

"Yes," agreed Trent, nodding, "I have been Ituria's friend for many years now, and I respect the rules of Middle Forest." Trent made a low growl and then continued, "Unfortunately, your new enemy, Ranco, does not."

Jenna wanted to know about Middle Forest and Ituria, things she didn't feel comfortable asking Ituria directly, and Trent would be able to answer some of the questions she had. But first, they needed to get Ituria back home, so he could rest and get better; her questions would have to wait for another time.

"Ituria has told me of the forest and its sections and rules. Can you help me get him back to his home in Middle Forest? He has been hurt and needs to rest. I don't think he would be able to win a fight with Ranco until he is better."

"You are in Middle Forest now," said Trent, looking around and then back at Jenna. "Ituria's home and his mate, Celeste, are only a few miles away. However, I know Ranco is prowling Middle Forest."

Trent made another low growling sound as he looked out into the darkness. "I heard him calling he was going to get a white wolf, so I came over to see what was happening. I tracked Ituria to the cave and saw you and some small animals, so I thought you must be taking care of him. You mentioned he was hurt, what happened? Did Ranco attack him?"

"No, Ranco did not get him, the human hunters did. He was shot in the leg, netted by the hunters, and locked in a cage. We were able to get him out, but Ranco saw us, and now is looking for us."

Trent seemed surprised at the series of events, and nodded his head, waiting for Jenna to continue. "The hunters chased Ranco from their camp," Jenna said, "not knowing we were rescuing Ituria. Do you know what might have happened to him?"

"The last I heard of Ranco," Trent answered, "he was running back to North Forest. He may have gone back to get his pack, I don't know. If he did, we need to hurry and get Ituria to a place where the Middle Forest animals can defend him. This small cave is not easy to protect. What animals do you have helping you?"

Jenna thought about her small group. None of them could fight a wolf and win. "I have a fox, two squirrels, and two small deer, not much help in a fight with a pack of wolves, unfortunately. They are good lookouts, though, and can fit into small places and run quickly."

Silent for a few moments, Trent was thinking deeply. Jenna wondered if he thought the situation was hopeless—what could a few small animals and two wolves do to defend the cave against a whole pack of wolves. He asked her, "What was Ituria's injury again? Is he able to fight?"

Jenna remembered the gash in his leg, and how it prevented him from running.

"He has a gash on his leg from the bullet; it kept him from running fast and does appear to cause him pain when he stands on it. He will need some time to heal before he can fight with us."

Trent looked at Jenna and was quiet again. He appeared deep in thought. Jenna wanted to know—*what he was thinking*? She waited for a few moments, and then asked, "Is there a chance we can get Ituria home without Ranco attacking us? Is it close enough?"

"It's several miles. If Ituria is having trouble walking, it might take a few hours. Being exposed in Middle Forest with Ranco and his pack for that long will be risky, but I will be glad to help guard him with you."

Jenna was relieved Trent would stay with them. "Thank you, I appreciate your assistance in getting Ituria home."

Trent tilted his head slightly as he looked at her again, and asked, "How long have you been in Middle Forest? I have not seen you here before."

Jenna hesitated to respond as she was not sure what she should tell this wolf. Just a few hours ago she was a girl in who lived in a house with her human family, and now she was a wolf trying to save the ruler of Middle Forest from a pack of vicious wolves.

What would he think of her if he knew the truth?

She couldn't tell him now; it would have to wait for another time. *What could she tell him?* It would have to be believable, as he would quickly see if she were making up some silly story. She tried to think, and could feel Trent staring at her intently, waiting for her answer.

"I am from the other side of what was East Forest, and I have not been to Middle Forest before," she said. "The residents from Middle Forest came to get me to help rescue their ruler, who was caught in a net. By the time we got to him, he was in a cage and Ranco was going to attack us. I am new to this forest, so I am not sure of the rules here."

Jenna hoped this would be enough to satisfy Trent. But it just raised more questions with him. "Did Ituria seem surprised you were here to help him?" he asked.

Chapter Six

LEGEND OF THE WHITE WOLF

That was a strange question, and she hadn't really thought about it before. Ituria seemed grateful she was there, but not really surprised.

"I think he was thankful for the help in getting out of the cage. He didn't say anything about me personally, as I was with several of his other friends." Jenna wondered where these questions lead and was not sure if she wanted to know the answer.

Suddenly, Trent's voice grew serious. "I am only telling you this because it could help Ituria get back to his home. Did he mention the legend regarding the white wolf to you at all?"

Now Jenna was getting worried. "No…"

"I didn't think he would have," said Trent, standing up and starting to pace, as if trying to decide how to start. "He knows if it is true, it would be something you might feel compelled to do; you are not of Middle Forest, so should not have to face such a burden."

"Wait…" she said, now thoroughly confused, "What burden?"

"I will tell you, and then you will have to decide what you want to do. It is not something to accept lightly."

Taking a deep breath, Trent sat back down facing Jenna and started talking quietly. "There is a legend that has been passed down through the years that if the ruler of Middle Forest is in trouble, a white wolf would come to save him."

Jenna thought to herself, this was what the small animals had said when they met in the forest. *Is she the white wolf they were all talking about?*

Trent continued, "This white wolf would have a special gift, the ability to heal the ruler with its touch. The bad part is that whatever injuries the ruler suffered, they would be transferred to the wolf; while the injuries would heal within a few hours, the scars from the injuries would always remain."

Now Jenna was nervous, there was so much about Middle Forest she did not know. How could she be a part of it, and how could they know she would be here? She had never gone into the forest before, only watched it from her back yard. What did these creatures know that she didn't?

Ralphie had mentioned a legend, but she hadn't really paid attention; now Trent was saying the same thing. *Was she supposed to be here—as a wolf— as part of Middle Forest?* What about her human family at home? Trent's voice interrupted her rambling thoughts.

"I don't know if this legend is true," said Trent, "but I haven't seen a white wolf in Middle Forest before, and now you are here rescuing Ituria, so it must have some truth to it."

Now it was Jenna's turn to sit quietly and think. After a minute, she realized she needed to get back to Ituria. He had said not to be long talking with Trent, and she needed to get back to the cave and get some sleep before morning. She looked at Trent, and he was looking back at her, waiting for her response to his last statement.

"I will have to think about this carefully," she said. "So much has happened in the last few hours, I am not sure what my role is in Middle Forest."

Looking back at the cave, she knew she needed to get back there soon. "I very much appreciate your offer to get Ituria back to his home, and we will leave in the morning once it is light enough to see in the forest. For now, I will try and get some rest; it has been a long night."

Of course, Jenna didn't think she would get any sleep, but she needed time to try and sort things out.

Trent agreed, "Yes, you will need to rest if we are to get Ituria back in the morning. I will wait here for you. If Ituria is up to the journey, it is a few miles to the west and the path is an easy one to follow. I will remain on guard in case Ranco makes it back here and locates us."

Winding her way up to the cave through the bushes, she entered quietly. The smaller animals were sleeping, but Ituria was sitting up and waiting for her return.

"Did Trent know what had happened to Ranco?" he asked.

Jenna nodded as she walked over and sat down beside him.

"Yes, he thinks Ranco got away from the hunters and might have headed back to North Forest to get the rest of his pack. We are planning to leave at first light in the morning to get you back home. Trent says it is a few miles away. Do you think you can walk that far? We would need to hurry so as not to be a target of Ranco and his pack."

Ituria nodded. "Yes, I will be able to make it. My leg is much better now, after being able to rest it and get some food and water. We shall be able to make it back home in the morning."

Jenna was relieved to hear this. So much was going through her head about the legend, and what she, as a white wolf, was going to do that she couldn't think straight. She needed some sleep, and suddenly felt exhausted. She got up and walked over to the front of the cave, laying down and putting her head down on her paws.

Ituria asked quietly, "Did Trent ask you any questions about why you were here and where you came from?"

Jenna picked her head up and looked at Ituria.

"Yes," she said. "He said he had never seen a white wolf in Middle Forest before, and he wanted to know where I had come from." Jenna paused, and then continued slowly, "I did not know if I should tell him I was a human girl—as you and the other animals know—so I told him I was from the other side of what was East Forest. Should I have said something else?"

"No, you gave a good and honest answer." Ituria responded, shaking his head a few times. "Trent does not really trust humans, so it might cause a problem if he knew what your true form was. I know you are good, as I know Trent is good, but he does not know you yet, so cannot make this judgment."

Jenna then thought of the things Trent had told her about the legend. "Trent said there is a legend in Middle Forest about a white wolf coming to help you when you are in trouble. Can you tell me what that is all about?"

Jenna didn't know how much of what Trent said she would tell Ituria, and she would wait to see what Ituria would tell her.

Ituria sat silently for a moment, and then replied, "There is a legend of a white wolf who would come into Middle Forest if the ruler is in trouble. I guess Ralphie and Sedric, who had seen you from the edge of the forest, thought you were the one to rescue me, so they sought you out. I had seen you occasionally as I walked through Middle Forest and looked out onto the human lands, and you did have the shadow of a wolf around you, so I can understand their actions."

"It was fortunate for me they were right in seeking you out to help." Ituria hesitated, and then added, "Did Trent say anything else about the legend?"

Jenna looked away for a moment, and then back at Ituria.

"Yes." She said, hesitating a moment, and then continuing, "He told me the white wolf would be able to heal the ruler of Middle Forest—I'm not quite sure how—but the wolf would bear the scars of whatever injuries the ruler had. I don't really understand this part of your legend."

Ituria was quiet for a few moments, and then quietly explained. "That is part of the legend I have heard too. I did not mention it for several reasons—first, my injuries are not so bad; second, if they were bad enough that I needed help in healing them, trying to heal me might kill you." Jenna's jaw dropped and her eyes widened.

Pausing for a moment to let this new information on the legend sink in, he then continued, "You see, what might be a minor injury to a large creature such as myself, when transferred to a smaller creature, would be too much for the smaller creature. It would be a major injury it could die from, rather than be able to heal itself. This is something I could not ask of any of my friends, and I would not want you to attempt." In a lighter tone, he added, "Anyway, I am going to be fine, so you don't have to worry about making such a decision."

Thinking further and looking directly at Jenna, his voice turned serious again as he added, "But, you must promise me, if such a situation arose where someone would tell you to attempt to use your special power..."

Jenna started to ask, "But what if..."

Ituria shook his head to stop her questions, and continued, "Before you even think about trying this, promise me you will ask me first, as I—as ruler of Middle Forest—would be the only one who could give permission for such an attempt."

Jenna looked at him, nodded, and agreed, "I will seek your approval and guidance before doing anything."

Ituria looked relieved. He leaned back and relaxed a little. "Now it is time to get some sleep. We have only a few hours before morning, and we will need some rest if we are to make the trip home." Jenna nodded, put her head down on her front paws, and fell fast asleep.

Chapter Seven

A TRIP THROUGH MIDDLE FOREST

Jenna woke with a start; she was a little stiff from sleeping on the floor of a cave—she had to think twice—what was she doing sleeping on the floor of a cave? Then the events of the night before started to flood back into her mind, like a crazy dream. She looked around her—she saw a large unicorn sitting against a dark cave wall surrounded by several small animals, all sleeping quietly.

She looked down at her hands, which were still large white paws. She was here helping the ruler of Middle Forest return to his home, with the assistance of a large wolf and the animals who helped her rescue him. Jenna was totally awake now! She got up to stretch her legs and was thinking about getting a drink of water from the stream.

Looking through the bushes at the entrance of the cave, she saw Trent down by the stream, still sitting attentively. It was starting to get light outside, so she knew they would have to move soon. Turning around, she saw Ituria and the other animals stirring as well.

"Okay, everyone," she said quietly, "Trent from West Forest is outside and has agreed to help us get back to Ituria's home. He has been guarding the cave all night while we have rested." She watched as the two squirrels started heading to the front of the cave. "I will go down first to make sure nothing has changed, and then signal for you to follow me. We must be quiet, as we do not know what Ranco has been up to overnight."

"One thing to remember," Ituria said to everyone as they gathered at the front of the cave, "Although we know Jenna is a human girl transformed into a wolf, we should not mention this to Trent or any of the other Middle Forest animals during our journey. It could be dangerous for Jenna if any of our enemies found out, as they would use her human weaknesses against her. If asked, Jenna is from east of what was East Forest, and this is her first trip into Middle Forest. No other information is needed or should be given."

Ralphie and the other creatures looked at Ituria, and then each other, nodding in agreement. Jenna nodded as well; knowing they would protect her secret made her feel much better.

"Trent," she called quietly, "We are ready. I'll come down first."

Carefully and quietly, Jenna picked her way through the bushes and down to the stream; she was thirsty and put her face to the stream to get a quick drink of water. Lapping the water with her tongue seemed quite natural, although she wasn't sure why. It was sort of like licking an ice cream cone.

Then she looked at Trent and asked, "Has anything changed since last night? Any further word on Ranco?"

Trent shook his head, "Everything seems the same. Is your group ready to go?"

"Yes," Jenna said, "Everyone is ready. Ituria is feeling much better this morning and should be able to travel quickly. I can give the two squirrels a ride on my back to keep us moving quicker," Jenna suggested.

"That would be a good idea," Trent said. "They could also be lookouts while we are traveling. Let's call everyone down and make a plan."

Nodding to the animals in the cave, she signaled to them it was okay to come down to the stream. Ralphie came down first, then the two squirrels scampered down. Next came the two deer and Ituria, more slowly, picking their way through the thick bushes.

Trent greeted them, "Good morning to you all." Bowing his head to Ituria, he continued, "Ituria, it is nice to meet with you again; I am sorry for the circumstances of our meeting. I have agreed to help the white wolf to get you back to your home. Are you doing well enough to make it back?"

Ituria nodded, "I am glad to see you, Trent, and agree these are not the best of circumstances. I'm well enough to make it home and thank you for your kind offer to assist us."

Trent then looked at Jenna and said, "White wolf, I'm sorry, but I did not get your name when we talked last night. If we are to be traveling together, it would be helpful to know."

Jenna looked around, "My name is Jenna," and then nodding to each of the animals as she introduced them, "The fox here is named Ralphie, the squirrels are Sedric and Fira, and the two deer are Evan and Frieda." Each animal nodded to Trent as they were introduced. "All of them have been helpful in getting Ituria away from the hunters and safe in the cave, and they will help us get him back to his home in Middle Forest."

"Pleased to make your acquaintance, animals of Middle Forest," said Trent. "Now we must make a quick plan and get moving. It is not good to stay out in the open for a long time."

"I will carry the squirrels on my back," said Jenna.

Trent nodded to Jenna and organized the rest of the group, "If I lead the way, Ituria, Ralphie, and the deer can follow me, and you, Jenna, can bring up the back. Sedric and Fira can watch both sides from your back, to let us know if anything is happening out of our line of sight. Let's be off now."

Trent turned and headed quickly into the forest. Ituria followed, limping slightly but able to keep up. Ralphie and the deer went next, followed by Jenna with Sedric and Fira on her back. They moved at a brisk pace and were soon back near the camp of the hunters. Trent slowed down, circling the camp, and stopped to make sure the rest of the group was with him.

Peering into the camp, Jenna saw it was empty; the hunters were gone. It looked like they would be back, though, as they had left their camping gear at the camp. She wondered if there was anything that might help them if Ranco should appear suddenly while they were on their way back. She motioned with her head toward the camp to let Trent know she wanted to take a quick look. Trent nodded and crouched on the ground, signaling the others to wait.

She carefully walked into the camp to see if there was anything helpful. There were the normal camping articles—including sleeping bags, cooking utensils, pans, matches, knifes, clothes, and rope. Jenna quickly grabbed a box of matches and a small pocketknife with her mouth—these were things Sedric and Fira could hold and headed back out of the camp. She also found a small bag and grabbed it too.

She whispered to Sedric, "These might come in handy later; please put the two items in the bag and hold on to them for me."

Looking at the small box and an oval-shaped hard rock, he wondered how they could help. But Jenna had been right about the shiny stick and how it opened the cage, so she must know about these things. He was able to put them into the small bag and put the bag over his shoulder so he could hold onto Jenna as she ran.

Jenna nodded to Trent that it was okay to continue, and the group took off again, with Trent in the lead, Jenna in the back, and Sedric and Fira on guard for possible danger. Heading deeper into the forest, the trees were getting taller and closer together, which slowed down their progress. There was a path for them to follow; however, this was both good and bad. It was easier to walk on the path, but much more dangerous, and Ranco could be waiting for them at any point along the way. They would have to be quick and careful.

Chapter Eight

THE HIDDEN PATH

They had traveled for about a half an hour when Trent suddenly stopped, got off the path and crouched on the ground. Ituria stopped and blended into the forest around him and vanished from sight, while the fox and deer immediately stopped and got into the woods beside the path. Quickly following Trent, Jenna crouched on the ground and the squirrels ran into the bushes. Trent was sniffing at the air; something must be close. He looked back but did not say anything.

The path was now clear, no trace of them was visible.

Jenna smelled something as well while they were waiting, but she didn't know what. She did not have the experience to identify the various smells of the forest her wolf nose could sense. Suddenly, she heard a noise, like a lot of people walking together, and peered through the bushes. These were not people as she knew them, but something more resembling a cross between a human and a deer, with a human top, but a bottom half covered with hair and hooves on their feet. The hair on their head was shoulder length and tousled, like it had never been combed, and there appeared to be two small horns sticking out of the tops of their heads.

There were five of them, talking and laughing as they walked down the path. Jenna didn't know what these were, but it was obvious Trent didn't want these creatures to know he and the others were nearby. Everyone stayed hidden until the other group of travelers were far down the path, and then Trent slowly came out of the bushes.

Standing beside Trent, she looked at him and whispered, "Who were they?"

"They were fauns," Trent explained, "They sometimes visit Middle Forest from their realm; however, they are not really helpful and can't be trusted. It is better they don't know we are here. If they knew, it would soon be known throughout the forest. While I and the other animals would not draw any attention, the sight of you and Ituria would get them talking to everyone they meet, which could cause us difficulties if they decide to talk to the wrong creatures."

Jenna nodded in agreement. The fewer who knew of their journey, the better. Soon they were on their way again. Trent indicated it was only another fifteen minutes or so until they reached Ituria's home in Middle Forest. Hoping they would make it without further incident, Jenna felt they couldn't get there soon enough.

Nevertheless, Jenna couldn't help but look at the trees, catching quick glimpses of other animals. Everything seemed more colorful and alive than what she had seen from the edge of the forest. The trees seemed more alive, something she could actually talk to; she wouldn't be surprised if they talked back to her, not here in Middle Forest. *What would you say to a tree if you knew it was listening?*

"Jenna," Sedric whispered, "are you daydreaming? You need to keep up with the others."

Jenna's mind had been wandering, and she was glad Sedric was paying attention.

"Thanks," she said, "everything is so different, I couldn't help but look around. I guess I should wait until we get Ituria back home."

Soon she caught up with the others, and in a few minutes, they were at the entrance to a big grove of trees. Stopping to gather the group together, Trent said, "We're almost to Ituria's home, and I will take him the rest of the way myself. There are magic paths through this part of the forest that will purposefully get you lost, and you might never be found. It is better Ituria and I go alone."

"Jenna, you and the others find a safe spot where you can keep a lookout until I return, it should only be a half-hour or so." Trent looked around and continued, "It might be best if you head up to the top of those large rocks; there might be a small cave, so you won't be out in the open."

Ituria agreed with Trent, "I have placed magical spells on the path from here to my home, to keep out invaders. Trent knows of these spells, and he will be safe as he has visited me on numerous occasions. Those who do not know how they work could be lost forever." Ituria bowed his head to each in the group as he continued, "Thank you again for rescuing me and helping me get home. Your help and courage are greatly appreciated. Please wait here for Trent; he will return soon."

Jenna and the others headed over to the rocky area, checking out the best places to hide until Trent came back. Looking at a cave about halfway up, Jenna asked, "Does everyone think they can make it up there? It looks safe, and we can see what is going on down on the path from there."

Nodding in agreement, they climbed up the rocks to the cave.

About the same size as the cave they had slept in the night before, there was plenty of room for everyone. Jenna checked to see if there might be something in the cave, but it appeared empty as far as the light would allow her to see. Everyone came in, and the smaller animals settled in for a short nap while Trent escorted Ituria back to his home.

They had gotten him back safely.

It was time to relax, but Jenna's wolf senses were on alert. She could not rest now, not until she saw Trent come back and confirm Ituria was safely back in his home. Positioning herself at the mouth of the cave overlooking the path, Jenna anxiously awaited Trent's return.

Chapter Nine

RANCO'S RETURN

The other animals had settled in for a short nap, but Jenna was too worried. She felt vulnerable without Trent and Ituria, not only for herself but her little friends. It was her duty to protect them, and she did not know if she would be able to do so.

What if Ranco came back, or some other creature of Middle Forest—she did not know who was to be trusted. Trent said he would not be long—only about half an hour—so she would wait at the entrance of the cave, keeping watch.

It was not long before she saw movement, maybe only ten minutes or so. She heard something and looked down at the path they had come from. Soon, she saw a large grey wolf, along with three other wolves, slowly walking up the path—their noses to the ground. The wolves stopped in front of the grove of trees Ituria and Trent had entered. Walking by the entrance, they stopped, circled, and came back. They circled a few times, always coming back to where Trent and Ituria went into the forest.

"This is where I lose their scent," said the large wolf quietly.

It was Ranco, Jenna realized. He had gone back to get part of his pack and had been tracking them. It was a good thing they had hurried; they had only been a few minutes ahead. What would he do now? What should she do?

"They could have gone into the trees," said one of the other wolves. "Should we check in there?"

"I don't know," Ranco replied. There was worry in his voice as he continued, "I've heard strange stories about animals going into this part of the forest and being lost for days—some were never seen again. I've heard that even if the path looks straight, it leads you around in circles. I don't know if that is true, but we will have to make a careful plan if we are going to find Ituria. Since Trent is with him, it will be more difficult. I don't smell that white wolf who helped him, so maybe it is no longer helping Ituria."

Jenna thought carefully, *she had been down there, on the same spot Ranco was standing.* Maybe because she was not a real wolf, she did not leave the scent of a wolf on the path. This might work to her advantage as they would not be looking for her now, only Trent and Ituria.

"We could just wait until they come out," said another of the wolves.

"That might work; there are only two of them," said Ranco, nodding his head. "We may wait for several hours, but they have to come back out sooner or later. Then we will be able to surprise them; we would have the advantage. Let's split into two, one set on each side, just off the path close to where they went into the trees. I'm sure they will be back some-time soon."

Ranco and one of the wolves went north a short way on the path and disappeared into the bushes. The other two went south and did the same. They were settling in to wait for someone to come out of the woods and were prepared to wait for hours.

Jenna realized Trent would probably come out of the forest in the next few minutes, and he would not stand a chance against four full-grown wolves. What could she do to warn him? She could send one of the little animals into the forest, they could make it past the wolves if they ran fast. No, the magic of the path would prevent them from finding Trent or Ituria. She needed to think. Carefully she backed into the cave and turned to look at the other animals. Sedric still had the small bag around his shoulder. It contained a knife and some matches—what could she do with those?

She had an idea. Quietly walking over to Sedric, who was napping, she gently nudged him with her nose to wake him. Once he opened his eyes, she whispered, "Ranco and some other wolves are hiding just off the path where Trent will be coming out. We need to warn him. Can you open the bag you have and find the small box?"

Sedric pulled out the box and was able to open it with his paws. In it, there were about 15 small wood sticks with red tops. Looking at Jenna, he whis-pered, "What can we do with these? They do not appear to be useful weapons, not against a wolf."

But Jenna had another plan. If they could light a small fire, the smoke in the air would warn Trent something was not right. The question was—where could they put a fire so it would not hurt them, but could be seen or smelled from the path leading away from Ituria's home?

First things first—the two squirrels would need to gather dried leaves and small twigs. While they were doing that, she would look around the outside of the cave to see if there was a little place where Ranco could not see them light the fire. "Sedric," whispered Jenna, "You and Fira need to find a few handfuls of leaves and twigs, they have to be dried and brown. I am going to try and light a fire to warn Trent. These small wood sticks will be able to help us start the fire."

Hearing the conversation, Fira hopped over as Jenna continued, "I don't think Ranco would think it suspicious for a few squirrels to be running around in the leaves and won't leave his spot watching the path. Just make sure you don't get near to them. If one does start chasing you, run up a tree, they can't follow you there. Make your pile of leaves just outside the cave to the north. There is a large bush that will hide what you are doing." Fira and Sedric nodded and ran off.

It took about five minutes for them to get a small

pile of leaves and twigs. Signaling for them to remain after their last trip, Jenna had them move the pile a little farther from the cave entrance. This spot would work for a small fire.

"Sedric," she said, "you will need to light the wood stick, as I am unable to do so. Do you see the dark stripe on the side of the box?" Sedric looked and nodded but didn't understand what he was supposed to do.

"I am going to hold the box with my paws, with the stripe facing up," Jenna said. "You need to take one of the wood sticks and pull the red part across the dark stripe quickly. As soon as you do, a fire will appear at the end, and you need to throw it onto the pile of leaves. The fire will burn, so don't touch it. Just throw the stick into the leaves. Do you understand?"

Looking at the small wood stick, and then at Jenna, Sedric shook his head. "Not really; I don't know how a stick can start a fire, but I will try."

Jenna nodded, and held the box between her paws, sitting close to the leaf pile. Sedric had one of the matches in his hand, and he pulled it across the dark stripe. Nothing happened. "You have to pull it faster and be ready to throw it into the pile," she whispered.

Sedric tried again, this time a small fire appeared at the end of the stick—he was so surprised he stared, amazed, as it started to burn down the stick. "Sedric," Jenna whispered urgently, "you must throw it into the leaves before you get burned!"

Quickly, he threw the stick into the leaves, and they started to burn too. Soon the small pile was burning, and a trail of smoke floated into the sky. Jenna hoped Trent would see the smoke, or at least smell it, and realize something was wrong.

The other animals had heard them, had come to the front of the cave, watched the fire burn, and the smoke trail up into the sky. They, too, hoped this would keep Trent safe. Now all they could do was wait.

Chapter Ten

TRAPPED

It was not long before Jenna saw a wolf on the path below them, but it was not Trent. It was Ranco, who must have smelled the smoke. As Jenna watched Ranco carefully walk up the path, she heard a sound from the sky. She looked up and saw a hawk circling overhead. It called out once more and turned to fly away.

Was this the same hawk who had been with them before? She was not sure but hoped it was going to get help, for now she and the others were trapped in the cave with Ranco searching around outside.

Jenna looked around from the front of the cave, up and down the rocks. There was no way to leave the cave without Ranco seeing them.

Ranco quietly called to his pack, "I smell smoke, but there was no lightning and I didn't hear any humans in the forest on our way here."

With a low growl, he continued, "We need to find out where it is coming from and how it started. I don't want to be trapped in a burning forest. You three wait for Trent and Ituria; I will check around to see where the smoke smell is coming from."

The wolves hesitated to return to their spots, looking at each other; one started to speak, "But…"

Ranco cut him off with a sharp bark, "No arguments! Call me if they return."

The three wolves nodded and went back to their hiding places in the forest, just on the outside of the path. Ranco started sniffing the air and sniffing the ground. He was going to find the source of the smoke and who made it.

Turning to look at the animals, Jenna motioned them to go to the back of the cave.

She carefully kicked some dirt on the fire to put it out and pushed the burned leaves a little farther away from the cave before joining them. The cave seemed to curve near the back, so they went around the turn where they could not be seen from the front of the cave.

They could not see where they were going, so they carefully felt their way, going slowly farther back into the cave. When they were fully hidden from the front, they stopped, silent, and listening to hear if they would be discovered.

It was not long before they could hear some movement at the front of the cave. No one moved. Whoever it was, they stopped in front of the cave and sniffed, and moved off a little to sniff where the fire had been. Jenna hoped the smoke would conceal their smell as there was a smell of smoke in the cave and on their fur. Huddling together in the darkness, they dared not make a sound.

After what seemed like hours, whoever was at the front of the cave moved away, and Jenna could hear the rattle of pebbles as the visitor went back down to the path. A minute later, she heard Ranco talking to his wolves. Moving near the front of the cave, she strained to hear what they were saying.

"I found the source of the smoke," he was reporting in low growls. "It looks like a human had started a fire and then put it out. There was the faint smell of a human up by the cave near the fire, but there was a bit of smoke around the cave, so I couldn't tell how many. They must be gone now, or we would hear or smell them. There was no camp set up, so they must have been passing through."

"Should we leave?" said one of the wolves.

"Not right now," said Ranco. "I'm not so worried about a human or two, and I don't want to lose Trent and Ituria. This is our best chance to catch them by surprise."

He sniffed around. "Let's go back to our original plan but be aware of any unusual smells or sounds that might indicate a human might be in the area."

Now they were worse off than before, thought Jenna. She and the other animals were trapped in the cave.

The fire was out, so they wouldn't be able to warn Trent of the ambush waiting for him when he came out of the trees.

One thing she had learned, though, was to a wolf, she smelled more like a human. She wondered if Trent had noticed. He must have, yet he didn't say anything to her about it. She wondered why.

Suddenly, she heard a slight noise from the back of the cave. Ralphie was moving back toward the front of the cave to join her. She nodded at him, and he sat down beside her. They both looked down at the path.

Looking at Ralphie, Jenna whispered, "Ranco and one of his wolves are waiting on the north side of the path, and two other wolves are waiting on the south side of the path. When Trent comes back out, they are planning to attack him. I don't know what we can do, as we are trapped in this cave ourselves."

Ralphie whispered back, "I have gone back in the cave, and it is bigger than we thought. It might have another opening somewhere if we go back far enough."

Ralphie paused, and slowly added, "The only problem is we can't see where we are going. We are feeling the floor and following it around, but we don't know if we are going in circles or what. Do you have any suggestions?"

Jenna thought carefully. If there was a back way out of the cave, they could get away from Ranco, and possibly warn Trent somehow.

But the cave was dark, and they couldn't see where it went. Jenna had an idea. What if the animals formed a chain and walked along the wall; they wouldn't be covering the same area again and again. They could follow the wall until it led them out, or until they came back to the front on the other side of the cave.

"Okay," said Jenna, "since we can't go out the front way, let's see if there is a back way. Let's go to the back on the right side of the cave," she called as she got up and headed toward the darkness behind them. "We can follow each other, and if there is no exit, we will end back up on the left side of the cave."

"Ralphie," she whispered as she stopped him for a moment, "I want you to go first, since you have a good sense of smell and can possibly smell any changes in the cave such as an opening. I'll put Sedric and Fira on my back, and we'll keep the deer between us. Let's go back and tell the others of our plan."

Ralphie nodded in agreement.

Jenna and Ralphie joined the others at the back of the cave. They discussed going to look for a back exit and needing to stay touching one another so they didn't get separated. Although the deer were a little afraid, they were glad they would be in the middle, so Ralphie and Jenna would be able to protect them.

The party formed what to Jenna looked like a small animal train. Ralphie was in the front, Evan had Ralphie's long foxtail in his mouth, Frieda had Evan's short tail in her mouth, Jenna had Frieda's short tail in her mouth, and Sedric and Fira were on her back—this was the only way they could keep in contact with each other in the dark.

Off they went into the darkness, with Ralphie's side pressed up against the right side of the cave. After only a few steps past the curve of the cave, they were in total darkness. Using only their sense of touch to guide them, they followed Ralphie's lead, with the larger animals leaning against the wall and making sure not to lose contact with each other.

Walking along this way for several minutes, Ralphie whispered, "I think I smell something; not sure what, so I'm going to go a little slower until I figure it out."

As a group, they moved slower in the cave, leaning against the right wall, which was a little damp now—like a fine mist had been sprayed on it. Jenna started to smell something too, but was also not sure what it was. It was a heavy smell—like hay, and a bit musty, like a stable where large animals are kept. Suddenly Ralphie stopped—and started to push backward, making everyone bunch up in confusion.

Ralphie whispered urgently, "I've just touched something that isn't a wall—we need to get out of here!" But before they could turn around, they heard movement from farther ahead of them in the cave.

"Who dares to enter the dragon's lair?" questioned a low rumbling voice.

Nobody moved. Total silence and darkness surrounded them all.

"I said, who dares to enter the dragon's lair?" this time much louder and with the sound of annoyance.

Jenna's mind was racing—*a dragon? Weren't they just pretend?* But she remembered she had seen some half-human creatures, and Ituria himself was a mythical creature. Since the dragon knew they were in his cave, they would have to do something, but what? Now they were trapped at both ends of the cave. Jenna tried to think hard—*what do dragons eat?* She was not sure she wanted to know the answer.

Chapter Eleven

TRUE IDENTITIES

J enna decided the best way was to answer and hope they could get away while they were talking to this creature.

"I am Jenna, a wolf from east of East Forest. With me are creatures from Middle Forest—Ralphie the fox, Sedric and Fira are squirrels, and Evan and Frieda are small deer, also from Middle Forest."

Jenna hoped what she had heard about Middle Forest was correct, and the animals who lived there did not prey on the other Middle Forest creatures. She waited for a reply.

Instead of a voice, she heard something sniffing the air and moving around in the darkness. Because the cave was so dark, or, because her wolf senses were better than her human senses, she could almost feel this was a huge creature, and it was moving closer to them in the darkness. What should they do now?

"Do you tell the truth?" challenged the voice. "Each of you, identify yourself. Step away from the wall and state your name and where you reside."

Putting her front foot gently on Frieda's back leg to keep contact, Jenna whispered to the group, "Each of you, do what it says, but keep part of you touching one of us, so we don't lose you. Since we are holding onto each other's tail, Ralphie you go first, with Evan leaning against the wall and holding onto your tail. Frieda, keep holding onto Evan's tail."

"Okay," said Ralphie to Jenna, his voice shaking. Ralphie moved away from the wall, Evan holding onto his tail. Into the darkness he said nervously, "I am Ralphie, I am a fox who lives in Middle Forest," and started to move back to the wall.

"Wait, stay where you are!" the voice commanded. Ralphie froze. The sound of something breathing deeply was heard, and they could feel it when the creature exhaled, like a small wind blowing through the cave.

"Greetings, Ralphie of Middle Forest," it said, "I have smelled you in the forest before, you are safe in my lair." The voice was gentle as it spoke to Ralphie, but it was not ready to lower its guard against this group. "Next!" it commanded.

Jenna whispered to Ralphie, "Ralphie, when you get back to the wall, hold onto Evan's back leg. Frieda, find and grab Ralphie's tail with your mouth, so Ralphie can be touching Evan."

There was a shifting of positions by the group, and shortly Evan was able to step away from the wall without losing touch with the others. "I am Evan, a deer who lives in Middle Forest." Evan was trembling, but stood still, now knowing the owner of this cave was going to smell him to identify him. Again, there was a small wind going through the cave, an inhale, and exhale from its owner.

"Greetings, Evan of Middle Forest, you too are safe in my lair." At this Evan quickly backed up, nearly knocking down the others.

After another round of shuffling, it was Frieda's turn. Frieda, the quietest of the bunch, slowly stepped away from the wall, with Ralphie holding gently holding her back leg in his mouth.

Silence. She was too afraid to speak, the only sounds to come out of her mouth were small breaths and a few squeaks.

Jenna spoke up, "Creature, this is Frieda, she is too afraid in the dark to speak."

"Silence!" it roared. "Only the one I am speaking to shall speak back to me." In a much calmer voice, the creature addressed Frieda. "Small creature, please do not be afraid of me. I think I have smelled you here in the forest before, but only want to know your name. Please, what is your name?"

Everyone waited. Slowly, Frieda tried to speak,

"My … name … is … Frieda." That was all she could say. Again, the small wind went through the cave, the creature inhaling and exhaling.

After a moment it said to her in a quiet voice, "Greetings, Frieda. You are from Middle Forest, and you are welcome in my cave. You may join your friends now." Then, in a deeper voice, it demanded, "Next!"

Now it was time for the squirrels—how would they manage to keep touch with these small creatures yet let them step away from the wall. After a lot more shuffling, Sedric was ready to introduce himself.

"I am Sedric," he said, "I am a squirrel who lives in the Middle Forest." Sedric stood there, waiting for the soft wind to come. As with the others, the creature gently sniffed him and responded, "Greetings, Sedric, you are from Middle Forest, and are safe in my lair."

Another round of shuffling, and it was Fira's turn. "I am Fira, a squirrel from Middle Forest."

After sniffing her, the creature responded calmly, "Greetings, Fira, you are a resident of Middle Forest and are safe in my lair." But its voice quickly changed to a command, "Who is next? Please stand forward and identify yourself!"

Ralphie grabbed hold of Jenna's tail, and the other creatures held on to him. Jenna stepped forward. Before speaking, Jenna thought—*would she be safe if she were not from Middle Forest?* What could she say so the creature would understand she was not a threat to it? She responded, "I am Jenna, a wolf from east of East Forest. I have come to Middle Forest to visit with Ituria." Standing still, she waited for a response.

The small wind of the creature's breathing swept through the cave, once—twice—three times. Jenna sensed the creature was moving closer, but did not dare move, as it could sense what they were doing.

"You lie!" it shouted. "You are not safe in my lair! Tell me now why I should not eat you where you stand, you have one minute to explain why you would lie to me!"

Jenna thought quickly—what had she said? What was a lie? Then she remembered when Ranco had smelled the cave and could not smell her scent. In the total darkness, the only thing this creature would have to identify her was her smell, and it was not the scent of a wolf.

Jenna spoke to the creature. "Pardon please, but I think I understand. I mean you no harm, nor anyone in Middle Forest. While in Middle Forest, I am in the shape of a wolf, but while living in East Forest, I am a human."

"Now you tell the truth," it said softly. "Thank you."

Jenna did not know what to do next, and she stood there waiting for the creature's next action. If it chose to eat her, there was not much she could do; she could not see it, and it moved quickly through its cave.

She waited for what seemed like hours, but it was only a minute or two.

"Greetings, Jenna of East Forest. I am Knocker, the dragon of Middle Forest. You are all safe in my cave, but I would like to know why you are here? I usually sleep for weeks at a time, and I was not planning to awaken for another few days. Why do you want to visit Ituria?"

Chapter Twelve

THE DRAGON PATROL

It was Ralphie who spoke up first. "Jenna helped us rescue Ituria from the hunters. We asked her to come help us; now we are trapped in this cave by Ranco, who is waiting to ambush Trent, and don't know what to do." Ralphie sounded stressed and was talking quickly.

Jenna thought a little more explaining would help, so she added, "We rescued Ituria—who had been injured—from a hunter's cage. Ranco saw us and got others from his pack and has returned to Middle Forest. Trent, from West Forest, helped us to get Ituria back home, and is walking him through the enchanted path. Now Ranco is waiting outside of Ituria's path to attack Trent when he returns. We indeed are trapped in this cave because Ranco will see us if we attempt to leave. We were looking for a back exit when we encountered you."

"This is indeed a puzzling situation," said Knocker. "You say Ituria is injured, what happened?"

"He was hit by one of the hunters' guns in the leg, but is doing much better, thanks to these creatures, who helped save him and got him food and water," said Jenna.

"I am grateful to all of you," he replied, "as Ituria is a good friend of mine. As you probably figured out, I am one of the creatures who protects Ituria and Middle Forest from invaders. That is why my cave is in front of the entrance to Ituria's home. And it is also why I was concerned with a human claiming to be a wolf saying she was looking for Ituria."

He continued, "Just so you know, Jenna, I do not eat meat, so would not have eaten you. I just wanted to frighten you into telling me the truth."

Knocker was much friendlier now, and his voice was calm. "Ituria has arranged several large fruit trees near my lair, so I am never without food. A dragon does need to eat a lot of food—at least one of my size." The dragon chuckled to himself. "I am a lot larger than you might imagine, if you have never seen a dragon before."

"Now," said Knocker, "Let's get to the business at hand. We need to get all of you out of the cave without Ranco or his wolves seeing you, and we need to meet up with Trent before he comes back out of the forest. Any suggestions?"

Sedric said, "We were looking for a back way out of the cave when we found you, is there a back way?"

"No," said Knocker, "My cave has only one entrance. Keeps it warm and allows me to sleep undisturbed. We will have to go out the front entrance. How many wolves are there and where are they located?"

Jenna spoke up, her voice shaking a little as she remembered the wolves waiting outside, "There are four wolves in all, two hidden on each side of the path leading to Ituria's home. They are hiding in the bushes and can't be seen from the path itself."

"Okay," said Knocker calmly, "here is what I propose—I will go out of the cave first, causing a little diversion, while the rest of you go behind me and slip down the rocks, heading south. If Ranco runs, he will go north toward his home. Stay hidden in the forest, but follow next to the path, and I will catch up with you shortly. You will hear me coming, as I seem to knock into trees a bit—that's where I got my name." Knocker chuckled again.

Jenna couldn't imagine what this dragon looked like, and how big could it be to hide them from the path?

"First we need to get to the front of the cave, so we can see where we are going," noted Ralphie. "Our only connection with the cave is leaning up against the wall. We will need to turn around and start toward the front."

Knocker snorted, "Nonsense, I will come over near you, and all of you will climb on my back, and I'll carry you out of here."

Suddenly there was a swishing in the cave, and they could hear a noise coming rapidly closer. Jenna was worried about this suggestion.

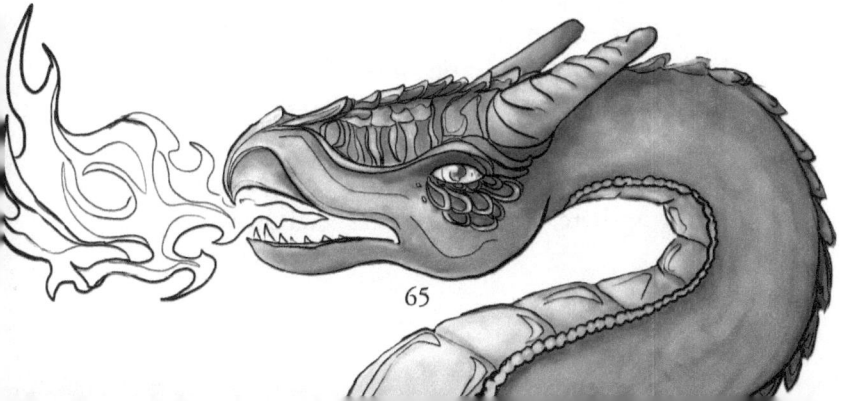

"Knocker," she said quickly, "since you are so big and do have a habit of knocking into things, it might be best if we went out separately. Some of us are tiny and would get hurt if you accidentally bumped us against the wall."

"I see your point," he said, and the swishing noises stopped. "I agree. Everyone, turn around and grab the one in front of you. Jenna, you and the squirrels will be first, then the two deer, with Ralphie bringing up the rear. Stay next to the same wall where you came in, and I will keep to the other side, so we won't meet in the dark. Let's go!"

Jenna could tell this dragon feared nothing, and she was glad. Shifting around and still leaning against the wall, they started following it out. Soon she could see some light in the distance and could hear beside them the movement coming from the dragon. As they got closer to the opening, she could start to see the outline of an enormous creature.

How would she describe the shape she was starting to see? While she had seen drawings of imagined dragons, this was totally different.

It was long and lean—like a large lizard—with four large feet, each with sharp claws. The neck was stretching forward, as if he didn't want to hit his head on the roof of the cave.

As it got lighter in the cave, she could see it had large wings—very impressive. Knocker's head was large, with a mouth full of sharp teeth, which at this point turned and looked at her.

"Jenna," he said quietly, "the cave gets a little narrower up here, so I will go first. Gather your group near the mouth of the cave. I will go out of the cave and make what I call my wake-up speech—letting Middle Forest know I'm around—and will flap my wings when you are safe to sneak by to my left and head into the woods."

Jenna nodded, and Knocker quickly slipped by them, exiting the cave. She thought even though he was so large, he moved quickly. She was glad they were friends. With this thought in mind, Jenna gathered the others near the front of the cave and waited for Knocker to start his speech.

"Greetings, creatures of Middle Forest," he called out, his voice booming through the trees. "It is I, Knocker, and I have awakened from my nap, and am here once again to protect you. All creatures of Middle Forest are safe, for I am your protector."

He paused for effect.

"Please be aware I will be patrolling the forest to seek out anyone who might harm you, and I might not see you if you are small, so please call to me or move if you hear me coming, so I do not step on you."

"To all creatures who are not from Middle Forest," he continued in an even louder voice, "This is fair warning I do not tolerate anyone who means harm to my creatures. I have permission from Ituria himself to eat any creature I feel to be a threat. Consider yourself warned, as I do not give a second warning once I start my patrol. As an update to all about the human who was wandering around a little while ago, you don't have to worry about him anymore. He wandered into my cave and tried to cook something. He made a wonderful breakfast!"

With that statement, Knocker flapped his wings a few times, as if pleased with himself.

This was the signal to start their descent from the cave, so Jenna and the others crouched along the ground and inched their way forward. Knocker was right, there would be no trouble hiding behind him as they got down the rocks; he had positioned himself to shield the entire rock side from view to anyone on or near the path. They jumped down quietly and headed south into the woods, keeping the path in sight but not getting close enough to where they could be seen.

As they left the rocks, Jenna wondered what Ranco would think of Knocker and his speech. She didn't have too long to wait. Knocker started toward the path after he saw they were in the woods, sniffing the air and ground as he walked.

Suddenly, there was a loud howling from the pathway. Ranco was calling to his pack, "Retreat! We will regroup at the edge of North Forest! Hurry, we don't want to be his next meal!"

Knocker continued his patrol toward the path, and when he saw the wolves running north, he blew fire at them, scorching the tips of their tails. "Be warned, invaders of Middle Forest, Knocker is on patrol now, and I do not tolerate intruders! Do not come back or you shall be my next snack!"

After they were out of sight, Knocker turned onto the path and headed south.

Chapter Thirteen

TIME FOR A SWIM

Continuing down the path, Knocker looked behind him every few minutes to make sure Ranco and his group were not returning.

"Okay, it is safe to join me now." he called out.

Jenna and the others emerged onto the path, which previously had looked rather large to them. With Knocker standing on the path though, it was quite small, as he took up the entire width and was quite long, stretching far down the path.

Jenna couldn't help but be amazed at the beautiful blue-green color of Knocker's scales as they sparkled in the sun. He certainly was a magnificent creature, rightfully proud of himself as a protector of Ituria and Middle Forest.

"It is best if you walk in front of me, so I can see you on the path. As you can tell, there is not much room on either side, and I might accidentally bump you into a tree or something."

Knocker was right, of course, they couldn't walk beside him.

He continued, "there is a second entrance to Ituria's home just up the path—not known to many creatures. Everyone must be able to swim, though. If you can't swim, you may ride on my back."

Thinking to herself, Jenna knew she could swim as a human, but as a wolf, she wasn't sure. She was good at the doggie paddle, so probably this would work in her present form. The squirrels would need to ride on someone's back, and the rest should be able to swim. "All right," she said, "let's go, and let's hurry so we don't miss Trent, who may be on his way back to the path by now."

Knocker agreed, "Yes, let's hurry. It is only a few more minutes down the path."

The group—with its new member—headed down the path. As Knocker had indicated earlier, it was only a few minutes before he called ahead to the others.

"Everyone, stop and look to your left. See a large tree with a smooth trunk? This hides a small underground cave with a river running next to Ituria's home. Whoever is getting on my back, get on now. The rest of you, follow behind."

Sedric and Fira climbed up on Knocker's back, with a little help from Jenna. Knocker headed off the path and walked carefully around the tree. Just as he described, there was a cave, barely big enough to allow Knocker to enter.

There was nothing lighting up the cave, and Jenna was starting to have second thoughts about this. Could she swim in the dark? How would she know which way to go?

"Knocker," she said, "How will we see in the dark?"

"Good point," he replied. "I think it best if everyone gets on my back, and I will swim across the river. We will shortly be at Ituria's home. However, you must keep your heads down as much as possible, as this cave barely allows me to pass through."

Knocker kneeled, and the rest of the animals got on Knocker's back, not without some difficulty. The scales were a little slippery—not slimy—but like climbing on glass. Each of them grabbed hold of a part of his folded wings and positioned themselves as close to Knocker's body as they could. Knocker took off into the cave and waded into an underground river not much wider than Knocker himself. "Don't worry about anything, I've got it all under control."

Knocker swam down the river for about two or three minutes and exited the river on the other side.

Jenna could see shadows of plants and trees here, but nothing was familiar. It was getting lighter, so they must be making their way out of the cave.

"It is safe to get down now, if you wish," said Knocker.

"You are welcome to stay if you desire, but most creatures find it a little scary to slide all over my scales as I walk. What do you think, Jenna?"

Jenna slid down the side of the dragon, jumping the last few feet. "I would agree, Knocker. I think I will walk from here. Thank you for the ride over the river," she said politely. Glad she didn't have to swim in the dark, she was also glad to have her feet back on the ground.

"We should be at Ituria's home in a few minutes, and Trent should be there," said Knocker, "Follow me!"

Knocker started walking quickly through a narrow path in the woods, bumping trees on either side as he went. He wasn't trying to hit them, Jenna noted, it was that he was so large even staying to the middle of the path, he touched the trees. Jenna thought to herself that he was a large dragon indeed.

The others followed Knocker, with Jenna taking up the rear with Sedric on her back. Jenna could not help but look at the trees as they walked. Many of them had large, fruit-like objects hanging from them, but nothing she could identify.

Thinking of fruit made Jenna think of food, and she realized she was famished. She had not eaten anything yet today, and her stomach was starting to rumble. Remembering Knocker said there were lots of trees that had food for him to eat, she wondered if she could eat them too.

She watched the small deer in front of her, and her mind started calculating—if she took one by the neck and bit down hard, it would provide her with a good meal; it would not take much to capture one of them…

Jenna stopped walking—what was she thinking! The wolf thought process must be kicking in, figuring out where her next meal was coming from!

She shook her head to try and get those thoughts out and called out to Knocker, "Hey, Knocker, what is there to eat around here?"

Although she tried to sound calm, even to her the question seemed out of place. They were almost to Ituria's home; she should wait until she got there.

Everyone stopped and looked at Jenna, the smaller animals had frightened looks on their faces. Knocker glanced over his shoulder at Jenna with a quizzical look. Sedric, who was riding on Jenna's back, asked, "Jenna, are you okay?"

Jenna replied, a bit too quickly, trying to quell the panic she could see in the eyes of the others, "My stomach is kind of rumbling. I have not eaten since I came to Middle Forest, and Knocker said there were lots of edible fruits." Attempting to explain further her unusual outburst, she continued, "I was just looking at the trees to try and decide which ones we could eat. Don't worry, I can wait until after we find Trent and Ituria."

The smaller animals nodded and smiled, and she smiled back. Jenna was glad they didn't know what she had really been thinking only a few moments ago.

Maybe they were all hungry, as no one had eaten today. She really didn't think she could kill anything anyway, so she would be quite happy with whatever was edible.

She realized though, she would need to be careful of new ideas slipping into her thoughts, to make sure no one would get hurt by what her wolf instincts wanted her to do. *She was still a human inside after all, right?*

Chapter Fourteen

SNACK TIME

Knocker took a minute or so to turn his body around and reply to Jenna. "No need to wait. Most of the fruit you see hanging from the trees is edible. There are only a few you should not touch, let alone eat. I will point these out to you as we go. Please feel free to snack as we walk along, I always do."

Knocker reached up into a tall tree and picked two large fruits shaped like long, thin, red balloons. He handed one to Jenna and took a bite of the other himself.

"This plant," he said after chewing for a moment, "is what we call the hanging cherry tree. Rather than make many small fruits, it has been transformed to make large fruit that can be easily picked and eaten."

There are still pits in the middle, probably twenty or so, but I don't worry about them, they are small and eating the pits won't hurt you."

Holding the fruit on the ground between her two paws, Jenna took a bite. It did taste a lot like a cherry, a little sweeter and juicier than the ones she had tasted before. She chewed a little and found a pit in the cherry pulp. To her, it was a little big to swallow, so she spit it out.

What a mess this fruit made—after a few bites, Jenna's paws were stained by the cherry juice, and she was sure it was also dripping down her face.

"Would anyone else like a bite?" Looking around, everyone looked a little hesitant at first, but joined in by taking little bites off the piece she still held in her paws.

Jenna looked up at Knocker, "Do you have anything not so messy?"

"Of course," he replied, pointing to another plant. "The fruits from these plants are much crunchier and dry. I always refer to them as cruncher plants. I know they have another name, but I never remember it."

This plant was lower to the ground, so Jenna was able to take some of the fruit from it herself. The fruit was shaped like large grapes. Although it had a hard outer crust it felt light, like a cheese puff or popcorn did, so she took a bite.

Knocker was right, these were crunchy and delicious. Thinking what they reminded her of in the human world, she remembered those little cheese crackers she loved to snack on while watching TV.

Since she was hungry, they tasted great! Jenna got a few "crackers" down for all the smaller animals, and everyone sat down for a quick picnic. While they were eating, Jenna asked, "Knocker, how much longer before we get to Ituria's home?"

"Not much longer at all," he said. "Only a minute or two. I could see it from the path before you called us to stop. It even looked like Ituria and Trent were standing out front. But judging by your faces, I think everyone should wash up before we go to meet Ituria, Trent, and Celeste."

Everyone looked at each other; each had dark red juice dripping from their mouths, and their paws were also covered. Not a good way to present yourself to the ruler of Middle Forest!

Luckily, Knocker had a solution.

"Around here," he said, "there are plants called pitcher plants, and they are filled with water. I usually use them for drinking, but they are also good for washing up."

He nodded toward another group of plants. "There are a few over here that will work well. But you must be extremely careful to use only the pitcher plants."

"Why?" asked Jenna.

"There is a similar plant called the trapper plant, and its contents are not water, but a type of glue." Knocker's voice had a more serious tone as he continued. "Once stuck to the trapper plant, it is a slow and painful death, and there is not much I know to make it let go."

Everyone looked at Knocker with alarm, and he chuckled.

"Not to worry though," Knocker explained. "You can tell the difference by the shape of the plant. Pitcher plants hold water in long slender tubes while the trapper plants hold their glue in wide shallow bowls—much more tempting for those who are thirsty."

Jenna shook her head, there was much about this forest she did not know that could hurt her if she did something without thinking it through. She would have to pay far more attention from now on.

Knocker directed them to the pitcher plants, and they took turns dipping their paws into them and washing their faces. "Much more presentable," said Jenna looking at her companions. "Shall we continue?"

Knocker managed to turn around on the path again, and the group was on its way. Within a few minutes, they reached Ituria and Trent, who were standing outside of a large cave entrance. The two seemed in deep conversation but looked pleasantly surprised to see the varied group of animals come walking up the path.

"Greetings," said Knocker, "I am glad to see you both. I have brought those who claim to be your friends. If this is not so, please so advise and I will dispatch them immediately."

Chapter Fifteen

NEW FRIENDS

Jenna and the others looked quickly at Knocker, and Jenna realized no matter how nice Knocker might seem, he took his job as protector of Ituria seriously. He could easily kill all of them if he felt they were a threat and realized he had helped them so he could keep track of them while he verified their story with Ituria.

"Thank you, Knocker." Ituria's solemn tone held a hint of humor. "These are indeed my friends and I thank you for bringing them to my home."

Ituria's voice became more relaxed as he explained. "These creatures have rescued me from Ranco and a group of hunters who have both found their way into Middle Forest. Trent and I were discussing the dangers presently threatening the Middle Forest animals, and we would be grateful if you would join us to determine the best way to resolve these problems."

"I am at your service, and I would be glad to help in any way you wish," said Knocker, bowing a most graceful bow, despite his large size.

"It is good to see you again, Jenna," said Trent. "Very clever of you to light a fire to warn me not to come out of the forest. Skye saw the fire, went over to see what was happening, and came back to warn me."

"She told me there were several wolves waiting for me to step onto the path. Were it not for you and your small friends, I am sure Ranco and his pack would have killed me when I came out onto the path. I'm also glad you met up with Knocker; Skye said you appeared to be hiding in his cave."

"I'm relieved the fire worked," replied Jenna. "I was so worried Ranco and his wolves would get you, but we could not do anything else. If Ranco had seen us, he would have killed us all. By trying to escape from Ranco, we found Knocker, who was able to lead us here. For this we are grateful. Thank you, Knocker, for your help in meeting back up with our friends, and for assisting us in finding some great food."

Jenna wanted to be sure proper thanks had been given to Knocker, who was appreciative of her kind words, as he seemed almost to glow with pride on his work well done.

"I am always glad to be of service to friends of Ituria," he said, nodding to Jenna.

"Since everyone is expressing thanks, please let me add mine," said a beautiful unicorn walking out of the cave with a large hawk riding on her back.

While Ituria was certainly a magnificent creature, Celeste had a striking, feminine beauty. Her long, flowing mane seemed to float in the breeze as she approached. "I am Celeste, and I am grateful to all of you for your assistance in getting Ituria back to me. Thanks to our special herbs, his leg is almost better now."

Celeste turned to look at the hawk. "This is my good friend, Skye. She keeps an eye on things from above. I am thankful she was able to warn Trent about Ranco's scheme, as Trent is also a good friend of ours."

Now Jenna could place a name to the hawk she had seen—Skye. She was a beautiful hawk, large and brown, with a white front section covered with small brown spots. Skye had given her courage on several occasions.

"Thanks to you as well, Skye, for your help and encouragement, it was greatly appreciated."

Skye nodded to Jenna, and said, "I am glad I was able to help."

Celeste looked at the group. "Why don't we all go into the cave and get comfortable, it appears Ituria, Trent, and Knocker have some planning to do. There is food there for everyone, and you can find a place to rest."

Everyone nodded in agreement and began to follow her inside. Jenna hoped it was a large cave, especially if Knocker was joining them. Her last two experiences with caves worried her.

Knocker did not appear to be worried and motioned all the smaller creatures to go in before him, then he bent his head and stepped inside. Staying back with Trent and Ituria, she went in last, not knowing what she would find inside.

Chapter Sixteen

PLANNING A QUEST

O nce she stepped inside the doorway, she entered a big cavern-like room, and for some reason it was not dark, but had some type of lighting making it almost like walking into a house. As far as the size of the cave, Jenna had nothing to worry about. The ceiling was about twenty feet high, and she could see the cave stretched back for more than a hundred feet, then broke up into smaller caves.

Looking to the sides, the cave was at least fifty feet wide, and the sides of the cave were lined with piles of various items. Some of the piles looked like hay, one looked like nuts of various types, and there was even a pile of the "crackers" they had tasted on the way in.

The air was fresh, not heavy, so there must have been some type of ventilation system. Whatever she expected when she walked in, she was quite surprised and impressed.

On the left wall near the back of the cave, there was a waterfall coming from the roof to the floor creating a small stream flowing about half the length of the left wall; at that point it went under the wall and out of the cave. Jenna was amazed; there was everything one could want in this cave—food, water, shelter—truly a home fit for the ruler of Middle Forest.

"My forest friends help keep our food supplies stocked," said Celeste, "Please help yourself to whatever you want to eat, we have fresh water in the stream too. Once you have eaten, I can show you to some of the smaller caves lined with grass, so you can rest."

Apart from Ituria, Trent, and Knocker, all the animals went to the various piles to get some food. Jenna went to the "cracker" pile with Ralphie, Sedric and Fira went to eat nuts, and Frieda and Evan decided to go for the hay pile. While the others were eating, Ituria, Trent and Knocker talked quietly near the front of the cave. Jenna wasn't close enough to hear them, so after eating for a few minutes, she lapped up some water from the stream and walked up to the front of the cave.

"Do you mind if I listen?" she asked.

"Not at all," said Ituria, "We would welcome your input on how to deal with the two major threats to Middle Forest."

He paused a moment to look outside through the cave entrance. "As you can already guess, the first problem is Ranco, who has gotten bolder and bolder as the months go by since he became leader of the North Forest—coming into Middle Forest and killing my animal friends." He continued, his voice filled with sadness, "My friends have never been hunted before, so don't hide like most animals in other forests—this makes them easy prey. I was trying to track Ranco down to talk to him about his actions when I ran into the hunters."

Sadness shifted to apprehension. "This brings us to the second problem," he continued, "We have never had hunters come into Middle Forest before. There are some minor protective barriers to keep hunters out. Unfortunately, we need to make plans to first get them out of Middle Forest and then determine how to keep them out."

"Trent," said Ituria, "Do you have any thoughts why Ranco would feel it necessary to come into Middle Forest to hunt? Before he became leader, his pack always stayed in North Forest, and we never had to worry about them."

"I do not know," replied Trent shaking his head, "We have a plentiful food supply in West Forest, so do not have a need to hunt here. Maybe something has happened in North Forest to upset the natural balance."

"The only way to find out would be to go to North Forest, review the situation, and possibly talk with Ranco himself. Based on past encounters with Ranco, talking with him is probably not an option, as he would rather fight than discuss things."

"If we sent Knocker up there to talk with him, do you think this would work?" Ituria asked the group.

"They may not talk to me," replied Knocker, "as I did chase them out of Middle Forest and threaten to eat them if they came back. I may not be able to get close enough to speak to them."

Nodding to Knocker, Ituria continued, "It would be good if we had a party go to North Forest to check out the current situation there," said Ituria. "At that point we could better address the question of why he is invading Middle Forest and could also assess how many are in his pack, in case we need to devise a protective plan for ourselves."

Trent agreed with Ituria. "I could go to North Forest and determine the balance of prey animals to predators, and possibly Skye could determine how many wolves there are from the sky."

"I could not send you alone," said Ituria, "They are just as likely to kill you as talk to you. You must take someone on the ground with you. Unfortunately, if you took part of your pack, I am afraid Ranco would take it as a threat, and there would be a lot of needless killing."

"We need to convey we are not trying to hurt his pack, but only want to discover the reason for his attacks in Middle Forest." Concern filled Ituria's voice as he worried for the safety of his friend, "I don't want to put you in danger by asking you to go there alone."

Turning to look at Knocker, he continued. "Knocker, are you available to join Trent on this journey to North Forest?"

"It would be an honor," said Knocker. "I just had a nice nap and am at full strength to protect Trent if the need arises. If Trent is with me, he will be safe."

"We have a plan as to Ranco," stated Ituria. "Now we must discuss the hunters in Middle Forest. Knocker, what have we currently been using to keep humans out, and do we know if they are working?"

Knocker thought for a moment, and replied "At this time, several paths are enchanted and cause the humans to end up back at the entrance to the path without the humans realizing it. This has seemed to work for many years, keeping distracted wanderers from getting in."

"We also have placed various plants around the perimeter of the forest and the paths—those causing rashes or having large thorns," he continued. "This keeps the humans who stray off the path from getting too far and makes them want to leave."

"Further," said Knocker, "You have placed several squadrons of biting insects to patrol the borders and attack any humans who might get past the other barriers. I think it would be wise to check on the plants and insects to see if they are still in place. The enchanted paths would still be working until you release them, so they should be working now. I don't know if they need to be checked out, but it would not hurt to confirm nothing has changed."

"The hunters," noted Trent, "are in Middle Forest near its border with North Forest. I am wondering if they came down from North Forest. This could also explain the presence of Ranco here, if the hunters have been killing his food in North Forest."

"That does make sense. Does anyone have any ideas about what might work against the hunters who have found their way into Middle Forest?" asked Ituria. "We need to get them to leave, and not want to return."

"I could find them and chase them away—or even dispose of them," answered Knocker.

"It probably would not keep them out," said Jenna, adding her thoughts to the conversation. "Once they see you, Knocker, they would bring more humans in to catch you, as you would be a great trophy to them."

"If you killed them, other humans would come looking for those you killed. We will have to think of something not so dramatic to make them want to leave and not return. I don't know what this would be yet, but there must be something…"

Suddenly Jenna stopped talking as she realized everyone was looking at her. She thought she would just be listening to them, and now she was discussing this serious matter as one of them. Should she let them decide a plan alone and stay out of the discussion? She really wasn't part of this group; what were they thinking about her?

"Sorry," said Jenna quietly, a little embarrassed, "I didn't mean to interrupt your discussion."

"We have not had much experience with hunters in West Forest," said Trent, "possibly because there are few humans living near us. You must have more experience with humans over by East Forest, Jenna, as I don't really know how they think."

Ituria turned to Jenna, "Jenna, can you think of anything that might work against the humans, something to make them leave and keep them out?"

Jenna looked at Ituria, and next at Trent, and back to Ituria. She realized real wolves would not have much contact with humans, so she probably shouldn't know how to deal with humans, if she were a real wolf.

Jenna remembered Trent really didn't like humans, so what would happen if she started discussing things from a human point of view?

Chapter Seventeen

TRUTH REVEALED

I turia and Knocker knew Jenna was a human inside, but had Trent figured it out? Ituria would not have told him, but Knocker might. Jenna started to feel nervous, and she wasn't sure what to say. Should she try and work out a plan, or would it reveal to Trent who she really was?

She must have looked nervous, too, with the other three looking at her, waiting for a reply.

"Jenna," said Trent, "relax. Even though you did not tell me when we first met, I knew from your scent you were not a wolf and was perplexed as to how you came to look like a wolf. Because you were helping Ituria, I did not ask you at that time, and figured I would wait until you were ready and the time was proper to discuss it."

"Now seems the proper time to discuss this," Trent continued, looking at her, "although now, you do have a mixed scent, both of a wolf and a human." Trent leaned forward and sniffed the air around Jenna. "Things are still changing within you, and we all need to know what is happening with you in this form so we know how best to protect you should we encounter danger you have not yet encountered as a wolf."

"This is most interesting," agreed Knocker, "your scent is definitely changing. Jenna, do you feel any different—do you feel more like a human or more like a wolf?"

Jenna had to think for a few moments. So, Trent had known from the beginning. He had not said anything because of Ituria. This made sense to her, and she was glad it was out in the open now, at least between the four of them.

"I still feel like my human-self most of the time," she said, "however, there was a moment I felt some wolf-like thoughts try to take over. It was scary to me because I was hungry at the time and my mind started thinking about the best way to catch some food. Luckily, Knocker was able to locate some safe plants to eat and the feelings went away. I have only been a wolf since last night," she continued, "This was the first time I had thoughts I would not normally have as a human."

It dawned on Jenna what a strange conversation this was; she was talking to a dragon, a unicorn, and a wolf. "I know this doesn't relate to the serious problems you are discussing, but does anyone have any idea of how I became a wolf in the first place?"

There was another silence.

Jenna looked from Ituria to Trent to Knocker, hoping someone had an answer.

Ituria spoke first. "I think you were called by the animals to come help me," said Ituria, "and because I needed help, Middle Forest—which has magic powers of its own—allowed you to take this shape to best help me. Middle Forest and its creatures must have known of you for some time and realized you would be the one to help when needed."

"Will I always be this way?" asked Jenna. She thought of her mom, who would be looking for her by now, wondering what had happened to her. "Will I remain in Middle Forest, or will I return home? Things are still unclear to me. I really don't know how I fit into all the things happening here now…" Jenna stopped talking again, shaking her head, unable to continue with the jumbled-up thoughts going through her mind.

"Don't worry," said Ituria. "When it is time, the magic of Middle Forest will change you back so you can return to your family. I think you are still in wolf form because Middle Forest needs your help to rid itself of the hunters, and you would have the most insight into how they think. This will help us to get them out and keep them out. Also, if you were in human form, we could not talk with you to get your help."

Jenna nodded slowly. "That makes sense," she replied quietly, almost to herself, "Once we have solved the problems here, I'll turn back into a human."

"Then back to the matters at hand," agreed Knocker, "How are we going to deal with the hunters? We need to have a plan before we take any action."

Jenna felt much better with the explanation Ituria had given. If she could help them get rid of the hunters, she would return to her human shape.

Jenna thought hard about what would keep her out of the forest, or any other place.

The insects, thorns and rash were a good start, but it would not bother some humans if they were searching for something.

Comfort wasn't something the hunters would worry about; they slept on the ground and ate whatever they could bring with them or catch. Something hunters would worry about was danger to themselves, or possibly if their trip was a waste of time.

"Different humans are afraid of different things," she concluded. "If we want to know what will scare these hunters away and keep them away, we will have to listen to them and determine what their fears are. I can take my friends and go back to the camp, stay just outside in the trees and listen to them talk, and we will have a much better idea what to do to make them go away."

"This does sound like a logical plan," said Ituria, "but I cannot let you go without some protection. Perhaps Trent can go with you until a plan is devised, and later he can join with Knocker to go to the edge of North Forest."

"I think you and Trent, along with the smaller animals, can get close to the hunters. However, and I think you will agree, Knocker will not be able to join the group without giving away your location. It is rather difficult for him to hide."

"This is true," said Knocker, "and the plan seems like it will work. Skye and I can make our way toward North Forest and wait for Trent before getting too close. The hunters' camp is on the way to

North Forest anyway, so we can start out together."
Looking at Trent, he continued, "Trent can accompany Jenna to the hunters' camp and work out a plan there to scare the hunters; then he can join me to talk with Ranco."

"I agree," said Ituria. "However, Jenna, you must remember you are not to go to North Forest with Trent and Knocker. You do not have the experience to fight and could get hurt. Knocker and Trent have fought together before and work well together. You will come back to my home once the hunters have been observed, and we will work out a plan for the hunters while Trent and Knocker talk with Ranco."

Jenna readily agreed. "I will return here." She felt relieved knowing she would not have to confront Ranco.

"Good luck to all," said Ituria, "and please keep yourselves safe!"

Chapter Eighteen

GOING BACK

Jenna woke the smaller animals to see if they wanted to join Trent and her. She wasn't sure if they were needed, but without them she would feel a little alone and lost, as they had been through so much together in such a short period of time.

They woke up and went to join Jenna near the stream. When they were all together, Jenna explained that to get the hunters to leave, they must go and listen to what the hunters were talking about, to figure out what might scare the hunters. Ralphie, Sedric, and Fira immediately volunteered to go, but the two deer were hesitant.

"Do we really need to go back to the hunters' camp?" Frieda asked softly. "They have guns and are so big. I was terrified the last time we were there. I don't understand what they say. Remember, only you, Jenna, will know what they are saying."

"This is true," said Jenna, "I would like the company and need some lookouts, but if you do not wish to go this time, I will understand."

Jenna gave the deer a nod of encouragement as she continued. "Once we have devised a plan to get rid of the hunters, we will check with you to see if you want to help. Do you want to stay here with Celeste until we come back?"

Frieda and Evan nodded shyly.

"It's not that we don't want to help," Evan said, trying to explain. "But we are small creatures and several of our friends have been killed by Ranco's pack and the hunters, so you can see why we are afraid. We do not have claws or teeth to fight with like you and Ralphie, nor can we climb trees to avoid danger, like Sedric and Fira. If we are spotted, they will kill us. We have no defense but to run, and they have guns to shoot us."

Jenna agreed. "I understand your reasoning. You stay here with Celeste until we return, so you will be safe. Ralphie, you can walk with me, and Sedric and Fira can ride on my back."

Trent and Knocker were already outside talking when Ralphie and Jenna walked out, Sedric and Fira on Jenna's back. They quietly went up to the others and stopped to let Trent and Knocker finish their conversation. Skye was perched on Knocker's shoulder.

"…I agree we should head north on the path," said Knocker, "but you will need to go into the forest after about half an hour. At that point, you and the others can sneak back to the hunters' camp."

"And you and Skye will wait on the path until I join you," agreed Trent, "We don't really want to hurt Ranco unless we must, and I am afraid seeing you might cause him to panic and attack. Skye can check on our progress, and once Jenna heads back to Ituria's home, I will join you."

Trent and Knocker nodded in agreement and turned to the others.

"The deer have decided to stay with Celeste and rest until we return," Jenna indicated. "They will help us once we have a plan."

"Glad you are with us, let's be off!" said Knocker. Looking at Jenna, he continued, "I will try and teach you some of the local plants as we walk by them; we will have about half an hour before your group will veer off the path into the deep forest."

They all set off to the north following the path. After a few minutes, Jenna turned to Knocker and spoke. "I was wondering if the trees around here have special powers. When we were coming down the path before, it was almost like they could sense I was near them, and if I talked to them, they would talk back, or is my imagination getting away from me?"

"Keen observation," stated Knocker, nodding, "Yes, you are quite correct. The trees near the center of Middle Forest can sense what is around them. Because they are plants, it is difficult for them to communicate with us, having a different language and all. However, if we pay close attention, they will respond to questions and give helpful information about others who have traveled the paths earlier."

"For example," continued Knocker, "we are coming to a large oak tree. It has been here for around a hundred years and has seen many things during its lifetime. Trees appreciate being respected for their knowledge and contributions, even though they can't convey it to you verbally."

"It is good to see you, mighty oak," greeted Knocker as he walked up to the tree, "We are glad to see you are so strong and tall today."

Jenna looked at the tree and was amazed as it appeared to straighten itself, standing a little taller, and even nodding slightly to Knocker as an acknowledgement of his greeting.

Was it only the wind? Or could the tree really be listening and responding to Knocker's words?

"This is Jenna," Knocker informed the tree, "she saw you on the way in and could feel your strength and awareness as she walked by. She is new to Middle Forest so did not know of all your abilities." Inclining his head to look at the squirrels and pointing, he continued, "And I believe you already know Sedric and Fira, who have enjoyed sharing your branches and the food you provide."

The tall tree seemed to turn to Jenna and the squirrels, and nod in acknowledgement to them too.

"We are grateful for your food and for allowing us to climb your branches," agreed Sedric. "You have helped us get through several winters."

"We thank you as well for your shade on the path in the summer," added Trent. "We shall talk again soon." Trent nodded his head in respect.

The tree was almost glowing at the acknowledgement of its contributions to the forest, and its leaves rustled in appreciation as the group continued on their way.

As they walked along, Knocker introduced Jenna to several other large trees; she was familiar with some of the types, but others she had never seen before.

Several had unusual fruit, some grew vines so long they touched the ground, creating a maze around their trunks, along with others, each with its own role to play in keeping the forest alive and well. Each tree was greeted with respect and responded to the kindness and gratitude expressed by Knocker and the others.

Knocker explained to Jenna some of the trees could make sounds in response to questions, but it really wasn't a formal language. Sometimes at night, others would rustle their leaves and make songs together, which helped the smaller animals get to sleep. Each of the trees had their own characteristics and ways of communicating, and it was all fascinating to Jenna.

In what seemed like only a few minutes, Knocker stopped.

"This is where we part. Skye and I will stay here and wait while the rest of you sneak near to the hunters' camp. Jenna, you are the only one who will understand what they are saying, but you mustn't try and communicate with the others—other than by small gestures—until you get away from the camp again. Any wolf howling or growling will immediately get the hunters to try and shoot or capture you, either of which would be bad for us all. Remember to stay as far away as you can while still being able to hear the hunters."

"Best of luck to you," wished Knocker as the party split. Knocker stood on the path with Skye on his shoulder, and the rest of the group headed into the woods.

Trent took the lead and seemed to know exactly where the hunters' camp was, quietly making his way toward it. Jenna was glad Trent was so confident, knowing this was not the time to ask any questions, just to follow him and let him find a safe hiding place for them all.

Within a few minutes, Jenna could hear noises in the distance: clanging of metal, breaking sticks, muffled talking—they must be getting closer. She was anxious as to how this would play out. Knowing they needed to get close enough to hear the hunters' conversation yet keep far enough away so the hunters would not be aware they were eavesdropping, she wondered if this was possible. This was not going to be an easy task!

Chapter Nineteen

EAVESDROPPING

Trent was walking slower now, keeping low on the ground, and leading them to a large clump of thick bushes. Jenna could see a fire had been lit a little farther on, possibly to cook some lunch. She nodded to Trent; this would be close enough for her to listen. Trent crouched down behind the bushes, Ralphie did the same beside him. Jenna sat down next to Ralphie, and the two squirrels got off her back and came closer to stand in front of Ralphie. They could just make out voices talking…

"…the place gives me the creeps," the first human was saying. "It's like even the trees are watching us. The sooner we get out of here, the better… how's lunch coming?" He looked nervously over his shoulder while waiting for an answer.

"Food's almost done," replied another human, stirring a pot over the fire. This was the older one who had the key. "We'll leave when we catch something to take home and not before," he grumbled.

"I know, Ike," the first human said. "But I still don't know how the horse got out of the cage; you had the key in your pocket when we went to sleep. I think this part of the forest is haunted or something…"

"Just your imagination, Joe," scoffed Ike. "I found the key outside the cage, so maybe I left it in the lock and the animal kicked the door. With a wolf crawling around, it would have spooked most animals, including horses." Then Ike's voice filled with wonder, "And what a horse, never seen one like that before. What a prize to take home; it would surely fetch a high price!"

"What do you think the thing was on his head?" asked Joe.

"It was a unicorn, it was," noted the third human, "and that was his golden horn. I read about them once. I never really believed in them 'til we caught this one."

"Oh, come on, Riley," Ike laughed. "Where did you come up such nonsense, some story book? There are no such things as unicorns. Next there will be dragons, and fairies, and ghosts popping out all over the place. Don't give Joe any ideas; he's spooked enough already."

"You got to admit though, there's something strange about this part of the forest; it is different from north of here." Riley paused, as if to emphasize the noises from the forest. "The plants look different, the animals act different, there are different sounds in the air…"

"Even I've started looking over my back as we walk through it. I almost expect a giant monster to pop out at us around every turn."

"What a trophy it would be!" Ike said sarcastically. "All right, stew's done. Put your bowls up. There you go." Ike passed out the stew from the pot and everyone started eating.

"Too bad we couldn't catch any meat for the stew," remarked Riley after a few minutes, "this stew is kind of plain with only some potatoes, carrots, and bacon."

"We're lucky to have what we have," said Ike. "My pocketknife and box of matches are missing. Luckily, I had a few matches in an old box with the pots," he said as he pointed to the supplies, "but I couldn't peel the vegetables; just cut them up with the machete. And my bag of salt is missing too, that's why it's not got much flavor. We'll have to look around when we're done, to see if some animal has knocked them off or hidden them under a bush or something."

"I sure hope we get something soon," said Joe quietly, "I'm ready to get out of here. What do you think we can get, Ike?"

"Well, we know there's wolves," replied Ike, "and smaller animals like deer and foxes, but I sure wish we could find that fancy horse again; it would be something to take home for sure."

Ike tapped his bowl as he contemplated his earnings.

"We would kill the others for skins and food, but that fancy horse—that fancy one I want alive. Make sure we pack the net for our afternoon hunt, Joe. I don't want to have to kill it … it's much more valuable if we keep it alive."

Ike finished up his meal and started packing his cooking gear.

"Pack everything up tight, boys," he told them. "We can't afford to lose anything else. Apparently, the little varmints around here can make things disappear." Ike chuckled.

"We'll be back tonight to rest, and we'll move camp tomorrow if we haven't found anything worth taking home."

Jenna nodded at Trent, it was time to go, while the hunters were occupied cleaning up camp. Quietly getting up, Trent turned and headed back toward the path, followed by the others. They moved quickly, but without making a sound, keeping low so the hunters would not see them leave.

It wasn't long before they were back at the path where Knocker and Skye were waiting. Knocker was eating some of the local fruit, and his face was a little messy from the juice running out of the fruit.

When he saw them coming, he leaned over to a small pitcher plant, and used his claw to scoop some water to wash his face.

"Remember, Jenna," he cautioned as they approached, "never use the trapper plant, see that flat plant over there, it's full of glue to trap and eat its prey. The pitcher plant is shaped like the trunk of a small tree and the water is safe for both drinking and washing."

Jenna nodded, "Thanks Knocker, I will remember. There are a lot of things to consider in trying to get rid of the hunters, and maybe it will come in useful. But now, they are done with their food and are on the hunt again. We need to get off the path as soon as possible. Ralphie, can you take me back to Ituria's home?"

Ralphie thought for a second and nodded, "Yes, I can bring you back to Ituria. Sedric and Fira can assist if I get a little lost, as they live close to his home. We will not go on the path but will stay close. The only problem would be the secret path to his home, how would we get through without getting lost?"

Trent spoke up, "I can take you back, but I think if I give you the proper instructions, you should be able to make it back without my help. Go in the main path entrance—it will almost immediately split into two paths. You must alternate turning right and left at each split in the path; keep track somehow as this is a maze, and if you make a wrong turn, you could wander around for days. Do you think you can do this, or should I lead you back?"

"I think we can do this," answered Ralphie, "if we are careful and keep track, we will make it."

"Good," said Jenna, "Trent, Knocker, and Skye can start their mission to visit North Forest and talk with Ranco. We will return to Ituria and work out a plan to get rid of the hunters."

Jenna turned to the three about to leave, "Good luck to you all, and please be careful," she said. "We will see you again soon with Ituria."

The parties went their separate ways; Trent, Knocker, and Skye heading to the north, with Jenna and the others working their way back to Ituria's home.

Ralphie went first through the secret path, and Sedric and Fira—who were riding on Jenna's back—kept close track of which way to turn. In about ten minutes, they found themselves back at Ituria's home, and the deer rushed out excitedly to greet them.

"Oh!" Frieda exclaimed, "We are so happy to see you; we were so worried about you. Where are the others?"

"They have gone to find Ranco and his pack up on the border of North Forest," explained Jenna. "We have listened to the hunters, and I think we can work out a plan to scare them out. Let's go inside and talk about what we can do as our part of protecting Middle Forest."

Chapter Twenty

MAKING PLANS

"**W**elcome back, my friends!" Ituria greeted them warmly as they got to the entrance of his cave, "What did you learn at the hunters' camp? Is there anything we can do to get them to leave?"

"I have been thinking of a few possibilities," Jenna replied, "but we will need everyone to help us get ready. Two of the hunters are already scared and believe in ghosts and haunted places. If we get them frightened enough, they will leave, and the other hunter will have to go too. It is the third human that will be the problem—he is out to make some money, and he said he won't let them leave until they catch something to sell; unless we can convince him to leave too."

Jenna turned and looked at Sedric.

"Sedric," she said, "what types of trees were we under? Would they be able to help us scare the hunters? Do they move or make noises or anything?"

"There were several oak trees, a few willows, and some pine trees," Sedric answered, "The oaks don't really make noises, but they can move a bit and will throw acorns if politely asked. The willows can move their branches a lot—they like to dance at night—and can make a low tone or whispering sound. The pine trees don't do too much, although they can drop some old branches if you ask them nicely."

"The trees may be able to help us scare the hunters. We'll need a lot more though, to make it work." Jenna turned to Ralphie and continued, "Ralphie, were there any bushes around to make bad smells or have stickers or thorns or anything?"

Knocker had talked about bushes used to repel intruders from Middle Forest, and she wondered if there were there any located around the hunters' camp.

"There were several thorny plants on the way to the camp," said Ralphie. "Usually, they keep their thorns in to protect themselves. Unless they feel threatened, they will not scratch, to conserve their resources. As far as other plants," Ralphie continued, "there are some that put off a stinky odor if something tries to eat them; they use little berry-like puffs of smell that chase most animals away."

Jenna nodded. "Maybe we could gather some of them up and crush them around the camp, to make it not so inviting."

She looked around at the others. "Also, maybe we could let the thorn plants know the hunters are dangerous to them, so they should make an extra effort to scratch and cut when the hunters go through."

Jenna started to pace, thinking of other options. "I am also thinking of asking the trees for help. The willows can make noise, maybe sing sad songs as they sway their branches. We can ask the oaks and pines to drop acorns and branches when the time is right."

Sedric's eyes followed Jenna intently as she paced back and forth, listening to her plans, and hoping he could help as well, even though he was small.

Jenna turned to look at Sedric, "Sedric, could you and Fira talk with the trees about what we need, as you can talk to them while the hunters are there? The hunters will not understand what you are saying."

"Of course," Sedric replied, "I am glad to help!"

"Also, did you see if the larger trees had any nest holes or anything?" asked Jenna. "Those might be used to further scare the hunters. What if we convinced the hunters the trees might eat them? Sedric, if you ran into one of the holes and came out covered with blood, they might think the tree had bitten you or something. We could use those cherry fruits to fake some blood, and the crunchy cracker plants to make it sound like the tree was really biting you. Do you think it would work?"

"I think you have the makings of a good plan," observed Ituria, nodding.

"What you need to do now is gather the necessary supplies and head back to the camp before they return. Although I agree the deer probably won't be able to help during the actual scaring process, they will be able to gather what you need and help transport it to the camp. I have the cherry fruit and … how did you say it, crunchy crackers, here in my cave, so you just need to figure out a way to transport them."

"We could use the pitcher plants," Jenna suggested, "empty out the water and use them as sort of holders for the crackers and cherry fruit."

Jenna remembered the trapper plants, and wondered if they would be useful? "What about the trapper plants? Could they help us?"

"What if you put the things you took from camp in the trapper plants," suggested Fira, "they would try to pick them up and get stuck themselves." Hopping over to Jenna, she continued, "They might also try to shake the glue off and shake it all over their camp. I have seen the liquid from a trapper plant eat through wood and fur, so it might cause damage to many of their items."

"What a great idea!" Jenna responded as she looked at Fira. "I saw those plants scattered around the forest on the way to the camp. If we have time, we will pull some over from closer to camp, so we don't get the glue on ourselves. We have to make sure only the hunters will be touched by the glue."

Turning to Ituria, Jenna continued, "Ituria, Knocker also mentioned biting insects. Can we get them to visit the camp this evening too, possibly following the hunters to camp and buzz around them?"

"It might be one more reason they would want to leave," agreed Ituria. "Okay, let's get started so you can get back to camp and set up before the hunters return."

Celeste went out and picked several large pitcher plants and brought them back to the cave. Sedric and Fira ran to the piles of hanging cherry fruit, filling two holders, and next to the piles of cracker plants, filling two with them as well. "This should be enough," they said as they put the last of the cracker snacks in the pitcher plant containers. "I think this will be more than enough for Jenna's plans. What else do we need?"

"We also need to get the stinky puffs off of those plants to scatter and smash around the camp," Jenna replied.

"Sedric and Fira, you will be talking to the trees and letting them know what we plan to do. You will need to explain that it is critical we obtain their help, as the plan will not work without them. Sedric, be sure to bring the small bag with you, we may need it." Sedric nodded and scampered over to grab the bag.

Turning to Ralphie, she continued, "Ralphie, on the way to camp, please let the thorn bushes know the hunters are not their friends and will hurt them if we allow them to stay. Talk to the stinging bugs as well. This is going to be a real battle, so we will need everything and every creature on our side if we are going to succeed."

"Evan and Frieda," said Jenna softly as she looked at the two frightened deer, "I know you don't want to be there when the hunters get back."

Evan and Frieda shook their heads.

"It would be much appreciated if you could help us by helping carry the supplies and smashing and sprinkling the puffy smelly stuff around the camp. When you are done, you can leave and let Celeste meet you at the front of the entrance to her home. With Celeste waiting, you wouldn't get lost on the path trying to return. Do you think you can do that?"

Evan and Frieda looked at each other and nodded quietly. "Thank you for understanding," replied Evan, "we do want to help, but feel by being there, we are only endangering ourselves and you, and aren't really much help to you as we can't fight, or climb trees, or anything."

"I will wait inside the path for you," agreed Celeste, "and will come out to meet you when I hear you on the path next to our house." Her warm voice gave them comfort.

"It will still be light enough for the two of you to get here, even if you stay just off the path so you won't be seen. Ituria will wait at the cave for word from Skye on how things are going to the north."

The trip back to the hunters' camp was quicker than they anticipated, with an urgency felt by everyone—they must be set up and hidden before the hunters' return.

After everything was set up and the hunters returned, it was Jenna's part to wait and listen to the hunters, and as their discussions indicated, to let the others know when to act. She would need to position herself in the bushes so the others could see her, but she could not be seen by the hunters.

As soon as they reached the camp, everyone scattered to start on their part of the work to be done to prepare for the hunters' return.

Chapter Twenty-One

PLANS IN MOTION

Looking around the campsite, Jenna remembered everything they had done this afternoon. She was glad they had completed their plans in time, but she worried if it would be enough.

Everything was completed, and all that was left was for the hunters to return and discover the little surprises the group had left around the camp. The deer had headed back and should be at Ituria's home by now; Celeste would be looking out for them to return.

It was getting dark, so the hunters would be returning soon for something to eat and to rest. Jenna had to concentrate on the task at hand—to make the hunters so uncomfortable or afraid they would leave the forest. She glanced at the squirrels and Ralphie; everyone was in place and hidden.

It was only a few minutes later when they heard the shuffling through the bushes as the hunters came toward the camp. Even though the humans were far off, there were occasional loud voices sounding like they were mad or yelling at something.

"…where did all of these thorns come from?" Jenna heard one of the humans say as they got closer.

"I don't remember such a hard time getting through the bushes before."

"Come on, Riley," replied another, "You're just tired and irritable. A good meal and a little rest will help. Joe, what did you end up getting to put in the stew for dinner?"

"I only got a few small birds, Ike." replied Joe. "It seemed like everything was hiding from us today. We'll have to pluck them, cut them up, and add them to the pot to simmer for a while. Hopefully, you'll find the salt bag so it will have a little flavor."

"Well, while you're plucking and cutting up the birds, I'll see if I can find the salt bag. It's got to be around here somewhere—maybe I can find my pocketknife too." Ike started mumbling to himself, but Jenna couldn't hear what he was saying.

Ike went over to the camping equipment and started moving things around. He picked up the pans and the small bag Jenna had taken before it fell out of the pan and onto the ground. Sedric had chewed a hole in the bottom, so all the salt fell onto the ground, mixing in with the dirt below.

"Darn varmints!" yelled Ike. "Now we have no salt. Something's chewed a hole in the bag and it's all mixed in with this dirt." Ike looked around the camp with a scowl on his face, "It better not be still hanging around here, or we'll be eating it for dinner!"

"Do you have any other flavorings we could use to go with the birds?" asked Joe. "Even a little pepper or something would be good."

"I didn't bring anything else, but sometimes I can find some spices and stuff growing in the woods to make the food better. I'll see if I can find something. Go ahead and start the fire, there's a few old matches left in the box next to the pot," Ike said as he walked off toward the trees.

Riley turned and looked at Joe once Ike got out of sight. "I'd sure like to get out of here," he said. "I don't even want to think about animals with sharp teeth coming into camp while we're sleeping."

"You know Ike won't leave without his prize," replied Joe as he gathered a few branches to start the fire. "He always has to have his trophy, no matter how long it takes."

"Did you notice the camp smells stinky tonight, do you think the critter that chewed up the salt bag left us another pile or something?" said Riley, "this will not be a comfortable place to sleep if it gets any worse."

"Maybe we can find the pile and get rid of it. I sure don't want to smell it all night."

Riley started walking around the camp, looking for what was making such a stinky smell. As he walked by the sleeping bags, the smell got stronger, so he unzipped his sleeping bag.

"Man ... Joe!" he exclaimed, looking into his bag, "Come look at this! Looks like something has decided to store all these awful smelly berries in my sleeping bag—oh, what a stench! I don't think I'll be able to get that stink out of my bag. I won't even be able to sleep on the top of it—where am I going to sleep tonight?"

"Empty them out and maybe it won't be so bad," encouraged Joe, "you will need to sleep somewhere. Maybe empty it and turn it over and sleep on the bottom where the berries haven't touched."

Suddenly, two squirrels ran across the camp and up a tree on the other side. They were chattering back and forth, running as fast as they could up the trunk. As they ran up the tree, the tree started moving, just a little bit, even though there was no wind. The two squirrels ran into a small knothole in the trunk.

Riley shook his head and looked at Joe, "This place was getting to me—what I need is a good meal and a good night's sleep. Joe, did you see the tree move, too? I know trees don't move by themselves, and the squirrels don't weigh enough to make any-thing move."

Joe looked back at Riley, "Don't get spooked. Things will be better in the morning. Come help me with dinner."

Riley nodded and walked back over to Joe to help with cleaning the birds. A few minutes later, they both jumped up as they heard Ike dashing back into the camp, dropping some plants he had gathered.

Ike was almost running, screaming the whole way, "Yeeeiii, the bugs are coming out, must be sunset. Get the bug spray—I hope someone brought bug spray. They are everywhere—they weren't near this bad last night. Ouch! They bite hard!"

Joe and Riley ran over to help Ike, brushing the bugs off his arms and legs. There seemed to be a giant swarm outside of the camp, buzzing around and around, almost like they were daring the hunters to come after them.

"Ike, I don't have any spray or anything, sorry."

Ike stomped away from the others, "Just leave me alone; I'm fine," he said, almost growling. "Let's get dinner cooking—did you get those birds cleaned? Where are the rest of the carrots? Let's have a good dinner. That's what we need!" He was angry and rambling.

Riley almost tripped running to the food bag to grab the carrots. He grabbed a handful, quickly broke them into several pieces, threw them into the stew pot, and added some water from the water jug.

"Did you find your knife to cut them up, Ike?" Joe asked gingerly, pointing to the small pile of cleaned birds, hoping Ike wouldn't get mad at him for asking.

"We plucked the birds but still need something to cut them with. The machete will make a mess of them—they are so small."

"No," muttered Ike, "I didn't find the knife." He was almost growling. "Just throw them in whole, and we'll break them apart after they're cooked."

Joe quickly got up and threw the birds into the pot with the carrots. He turned to Riley and quietly suggested, "Why don't you get your sleeping bag cleaned out? Maybe air it out on the branch of a tree, and maybe you will be able to use it tonight."

"What are you mumbling about over there?" barked Ike.

"Seems like some of the critters started storing some yucky berries in my sleeping bag, and I need to clean them out before I can sleep in it," replied Riley as he turned to Joe. "Good idea, Joe. I'll let it air out for a while. Maybe it will help!"

Riley shook the berries out of the sleeping bag and walked over to a tall pine tree near the camp. He threw it over the lowest branch and spread it out so it could get some air. He heard the squirrels chattering that he had seen earlier, and figured he must have disturbed their nest when he shook the tree to put the bag on it. "Too bad there's no breeze tonight; it would help a lot."

"What do you mean there's no breeze?" grumbled Ike. "Look at the branches of that pine moving back and forth. There's a storm heading this way, from the looks of it."

Joe and Riley got up and looked at the tree—then they looked at the other trees. "Ike," said Joe quietly, "look at the other trees. None of them are moving—only the tree Riley hung his sleeping bag on. That is really kind of spooky."

Ike got up and looked around the camp. He was in no mood for more problems. "It must be those squirrels running up and down the branches. Good thing it's not going to rain. Now check on the food. I'm getting hungry."

"I'm on it," said Joe, turning to Riley as he continued, "Why don't you take your bag off the tree and put it on the one a few down? The branch looks sturdier, and I would feel a whole lot less worried."

"Will do," said Riley and went to pull down the sleeping bag. The tree started shaking harder, and suddenly the two squirrels ran out of the hollow in the tree squealing loudly like they had been hurt or scared. It looked like there was blood on their fur, and Riley tried to look to see if they were fighting with each other. They weren't biting each other but quickly jumped to another tree. The squirrels seemed to be running away, but from what?

Riley looked back to the hole in the tree where the squirrels had come from—there was blood around the hole where the squirrels had run out—it was dripping down the trunk now. Was the tree alive? It seemed to be swaying and the branches moved, even though there was not a bit of a breeze.

Riley quickly grabbed his sleeping bag and backed toward Joe and Ike. "Hey guys!" he whispered, pointing to the tree, his fear causing him to panic. "There is something about this tree that is not right. Look, there is blood dripping out of it, down the trunk. And it's moving even when there's no wind!"

Chapter Twenty-Two

MORE MISCHIEF

"Riley, you have such an imagination," chided Ike. "Next you'll be telling me it's alive and going to grab us and eat us for dinner!" Ike chuckled, but it wasn't a heartfelt chuckle; he seemed to be getting a little worried himself.

Suddenly, the squirrels started chattering again, running up and down a large willow tree.

"Man, those things are crazy!" exclaimed Joe. "Let's just eat and maybe they'll go away!"

Riley went over to get some bowls and spoons and found a ladle to stir and serve the stew. He broke up the cooked birds. They were cooked and broke apart easily. Because Ike had thrown down the herbs he'd found as he tried to get the bugs off him, there were no herbs to flavor the food.

Riley spoke as he handed out the bowls, "I'm glad we have some meat in the stew tonight at least!"

Each of the men had a bowl now, and Riley was splitting up the stew between them all.

They ate quietly, each of them lost in their own thoughts. Riley looked around warily and said softly, "Man, I can't wait until tomorrow. I just want the night to be over. I've had enough of this craziness."

A strange sound made him stop chewing. "Joe, did you hear that?" he whispered quietly.

Riley listened without moving, and there was a crunching sound, barely audible, but it was there.

Joe looked at Riley. "What are you talking about?" he asked in a loud voice. "Is there something wrong with the stew?"

"No, listen." Riley put his finger to his mouth, motioning for Joe to listen. Both Joe and Riley stopped eating and were motionless, straining their ears to listen.

"You guys are spooking each other!" growled Ike, who kept eating as loudly as he could, banging his spoon on the bowl. But after a minute, Ike stopped eating too. All three of them sat quietly, listening. Every few seconds they could hear it. A small, crunching noise, and Joe remarked, "I never heard nothing like that before."

"All right!" yelled Ike. "Where is it coming from? It's something in the trees or in the tall grass over there. Rather than sit here scaring yourselves silly, go find out what it is!"

Joe and Riley looked at each other, then at Ike. Slowly, they got up and walked together toward the tall grass.

The crunching sound intensified, getting louder and faster. Joe and Riley stopped and backed away slowly, keeping their eyes on the tall grass, hoping nothing would jump out at them.

"I'm not going in there," said Riley, shaking his head, "Something got blood on the squirrels and the tree, and I don't want to know what it is. I'm going to get my sleeping bag off the ground and start packing—I'm getting out of this place before it's dark, and it's at least an hour's hike to get out of the forest."

Ike stood up and glared at Riley. "That's enough of that talk. Are you a baby? Can't take a few noises— have to run home to Mommy?" Ike walked quickly over to the tall grass and started grabbing into it with his hands. "Look, there's nothing in there to hurt you, you sissies!"

Suddenly, Ike got still and quiet, his hand still in the grass. As he slowly pulled his hand out, there was a large cut down the palm of his hand.

"What would to this?" he wondered, almost to himself, and got a dish cloth to wrap his hand, trying to stop the bleeding from the cut.

The crunching started again—slowly at first, gradually increasing in speed until there was a constant crunch echoing through the night. Not loud, but constant. As if on cue, the squirrels started chattering again, and ran around the trunk of the large willow tree. It seemed as if the tree itself was joining in with the squirrels with a low, barely audible moaning sound, and its branches were slowly moving down toward the men staring at it.

"That's enough!" said Joe. "There is no way we should be staying here tonight. Don't you see— there's something about this spot that doesn't want us here!" Joe was scared; he started grabbing things and throwing them in bags, packing up with great haste. As he packed, he said, "We should go. Let's head north and find a friendlier campsite."

Jenna had been directing the others up until now, but it was Jenna's turn to act—first, she made a low growl as she slowly crawled around the camp, crouching low so they could not see her. It got their attention.

The men looked around, trying to figure out where was it coming from. Their faces showed fear now, even Ike's eyes were wide and his mouth open just a little. It was easy to growl, Jenna found out. She would say, "Get out of here; leave the forest!" and other threatening statements, and the men would hear it as a wolf growl. Even to Jenna, who was talking as a wolf, it sounded frightening.

After a few minutes, she started to howl—a long loud howl—just like she remembered hearing wolves howl in the woods and on TV. She stopped for a few seconds as she circled the camp, and then howled again from a different position. Jenna hoped the hunters would think there was more than one wolf outside of the camp.

This was enough even for Ike. "Let's pack and go. Maybe we'll get one of those noisy wolves on the way out." Ike grabbed his gun and threw the strap over his shoulder. "Break camp and head north! We'll see how far we can get before we have to stop."

Riley joined Joe's efforts, and they quickly gathered everything laying around camp. Backpacks were packed, not neatly, but everything they brought was packed and ready to go in a matter of minutes. Ike was glaring out into the woods, hoping to get a shot at a wolf.

Jenna knew she had to stay out of his sight, and constantly moved to keep on the other side of camp from him.

"Let's go!" Ike ordered, holding his gun in front of him. "I'm going to be keeping my eye out for something to take home. You know I don't like going home empty handed!"

Chapter Twenty-Three

CONSEQUENCES

The hunters headed north, and Jenna and the other animals fell back behind them so they would not be seen. Jenna was happy they had been able to get the humans to leave but didn't want to say anything yet, afraid the hunters would hear them and come back.

Finally, when the hunters were far away, Jenna whispered "We did it! We got them to leave. You were all so great! Sedric, go tell the trees they did a great job too, and we do appreciate all their help."

Sedric ran off and everyone could hear him chattering to the pine and willow trees. The trees seemed to nod in return, gladly accepting the thanks for their part in the spectacle.

"Let's head on back to Ituria's home," suggested Jenna. "We can wait there for Trent and Knocker to get back from their meeting with Ranco. Sedric and Fira, why don't you jump on my back, and we'll be on our way."

They headed back toward Ituria's home, still being quite cautious to make sure the hunters had not stopped or turned around.

It took about half an hour to get back, and Jenna remembered to follow Celeste's instructions on not getting lost on the maze back to the cave.

"Celeste—Ituria!" Jenna called as she got closer. "We were able to get the hunters to leave; they are heading north. Any word from Trent or Knocker?"

"No," replied Ituria, stepping out from the cave. "We are still waiting to hear something. We are hoping to hear from them soon. While we are waiting, how did it go—are the hunters gone for good?"

"I don't know if they are gone for good, but they were not happy when they left," said Ralphie.

Before they could talk further, there was a screeching from the sky as Skye flew down and landed on Celeste's back.

"Ituria!" said Skye. "You must come quickly. The hunters left the woods through the North Forest, but before they left, they saw Trent and Ranco. Ranco was shot dead, and Trent is gravely wounded. Hurry, we must help him!"

"Lead the way, and we will follow. Go, Skye, and call out so if we lose sight of you, we can still follow!"

Everything had changed in an instant. Ituria took off with Jenna right behind. So long as Jenna kept Ituria in sight, she knew she would not get lost.

Jenna kept running through her mind the events of the day—was there anything she could have done to have prevented the hunters from shooting Trent? *Keep Trent from going to see Ranco—keep the hunters from going north*—her thoughts were racing. What could they do now? Surely Ituria had some answer to save him.

It only took a few minutes to get to Trent, but it seemed like forever. Trent was laying on the ground under a tree, bleeding heavily from his shoulder. Knocker appeared and lowered his head when he saw Ituria.

"Ituria, I am sorry," said Knocker. "I was unable to prevent Trent from being hurt. Trent and Ranco were ready to fight, and suddenly the hunters burst into the clearing. The hunter with the gun shot Ranco first, and then Trent before I could get to them. One roar from me sent them all running again, but it was too late. I am sorry."

"Knocker," murmured Trent, "it is not your fault. We all did what we had to do. You were to be hidden from Ranco, so couldn't see the hunters until it was too late. Do not blame yourself."

Jenna could tell Trent was weak and had lost a lot of blood.

"Ituria," she whispered, "how bad is he hurt?"

"I do not know for sure, but it looks pretty bad. He may not make it," Ituria whispered back. "I do not have any magic for bullets, unfortunately, so I cannot help him."

Jenna was heartbroken. Was there anything she could do? Could she, with the help of the others, try and bandage the wound and stop the bleeding? The squirrels were not here, and Jenna could not do anything with her wolf paws. But she could not let Trent die. *What can I do?*

"Ituria," she whispered urgently, "Trent is the ruler of West Forest. The legend says I can heal the ruler of the forest. Can I help him? You told me to ask you if I ever wanted to try. Please let me know if you think this is possible. If there is anything I can do, I will do it, as Trent has helped me so much."

"It is true," Ituria noted, "the white wolf is said to have the power to heal the ruler of Middle Forest…"

"What if I am to heal *a* ruler *in* Middle Forest—what if the legend means I shall heal not you, but Trent? Please tell me what I need to do! I do not want him to die…" Jenna was pleading now.

"Are you sure you want to attempt this?" said Ituria. "You will absorb the wound, and you will feel all of Trent's pain. You will only feel the pain for a few hours, but you will have the scar forever. Is this something you are willing to accept?"

Jenna looked over to Trent, and without a moment of hesitation, she answered.

"Yes," she calmly replied, "I *am* willing to accept the consequences. I believe this is why I am still a wolf and still in Middle Forest. This is what I am supposed to do, and I want to do so."

"Trent," Ituria called, "Jenna is going to try and help you. She understands the consequences and believes it is what she should do. Please lay still and we will do our best to help you get well."

Trent was barely conscious but did open his eyes and look at Jenna. He looked worried for her safety but was too weak to speak. Jenna knew she must do whatever she could to save such a noble animal. Jenna looked back at Ituria and nodded. They quickly went toward Trent together.

"We must hurry," Jenna urged. "I feel there is not much time!"

"Jenna, go to Trent, and put your paw gently on his shoulder where he is shot," instructed Ituria. "You must close your eyes and concentrate with all your thoughts to connect with Trent's thoughts. You must become one in mind with him—he is not strong, so you must be his strength. Go now. I agree there is not much time!"

Jenna sat next to Trent and gently laid her paw on his shoulder. The instant connection with Trent surprised her, but also encouraged her; this is what she should be doing.

She could feel Trent, barely breathing, struggling to stay alive. She closed her eyes and concentrated, like Ituria had said. She tried to feel Trent's thoughts and emotions—they were faint—he was just hanging on.

"Trent," she whispered, "send me your thoughts. Help me to help you. This is the way it is supposed to be."

Jenna continued to concentrate—she remembered the first time she saw Trent, the shadow down by the stream, not knowing whether he was a friend or enemy. She remembered how he led them to Ituria's home and how she knew he had to survive. Her thoughts were getting further away as she went into a trance.

She was seeing the cave from Trent's point of view—looking up to see Jenna at the front of the cave with Ituria. Jenna saw herself walk down to talk with Trent by the stream, talking about the situation and Ituria. She felt Trent's concern as he stayed up all night to protect them, and saw through Trent's eyes as they came down the hill the next morning.

Suddenly, Jenna felt a pain in her shoulder that was increasing. She did not know if she could hold on to Trent's shoulder. But she knew she must, because if she let go, Trent would die.

Jenna kept repeating to herself: *The pain will only last for a little while and will go away. It will go away. Hang on, it will go away…*

During the next few hours, Jenna drifted in and out of consciousness, overhearing things but not having enough strength to respond or even open her eyes.

She felt Knocker pick her up; his strong arms lifted her gently, but she didn't know where she was being carried. She heard Ituria talking with Trent, but she couldn't understand what they were saying. Then she fell into a deep sleep.

Chapter Twenty-Four

HOME AGAIN

Jenna turned over; she felt so tired, but knew it was time to get up. She tried to figure out where she was, was she still in the forest? Had Knocker carried her back to Ituria's cave? Where she was laying was soft, so she must be in somebody's home.

She tried opening her eyes. It was a struggle. When she finally opened them, she gasped.

She was back in her own room, the bed—windows—curtains—all the way they were before she'd left yesterday evening. She quickly looked down at her hands. They were human hands—not wolf paws. She was no longer covered with white hair. Could this have been just one big dream?

As Jenna went to sit up, she leaned on her shoulder—a twinge of pain shot through her arm, causing her to catch her breath. Jenna looked under her shirt and saw a scar about the size of a quarter on her shoulder in the same place Trent had been shot. So, it was real—she had absorbed Trent's wound. It was almost healed, with the scar remaining. But who would believe her?

Slowly her bedroom door opened, and a head peered into the darkened room. It was her older sister, Sandy. "Jenna, are you here? Are you back yet?" Sandy whispered.

"Sandy," answered Jenna, "I'm right here. What's going on?"

"I told Mom you weren't feeling well yesterday and just wanted to stay in bed and I brought you food," Sandy replied, pointing to several plates piled into the corner. "See the pile of food in the corner?"

This didn't sound like the sister Jenna remembered just a day ago, the one who was always so ready to order her around. Her sister sounded uncertain and confused.

"Last night…" Sandy started and then paused, not sure how to continue. "Last night, I saw you outside with a fox, and somehow you transformed into a wolf and ran into the forest. It was so weird and scary. How did you do it?" Her question came out quickly, and looking at Jenna, she took a deep breath and continued her side of the story.

"I figured I had better cover for you for a day or so if I could, or Mom would have everyone looking in the woods, shooting any wolf they saw, and they would shoot you!"

Jenna smiled at her sister's prophetic words.

"So, I made up the story you were sick, and since Mom had to work, I told her I would take care of you…" Now she was rambling.

Jenna jumped up and hugged her and held her tight, whispering, "Thanks, Sandy."

She had never felt this much love and appreciation for her sister. She had no idea if she could explain it all—or if her sister would even believe it, but things were different between them now. They both sat down on Jenna's bed as Sandy looked at Jenna, waiting for her to explain.

In that moment, Jenna knew she and Sandy would be much closer, and Jenna finally felt she could trust her sister. "I have such a story to tell you!"

As Jenna recounted her amazing journey to Sandy, Jenna wondered in the back of her mind if she would ever see her forest friends again, and if she would ever again experience the excitement and strength of being a white wolf.

She was glad she had done her part to help Ituria, Trent, and the others. She also knew she would always have friends in the forest, and only time would tell if they would need her help again.

NOTE FROM
THE AUTHOR

Although this is a fantasy fiction adventure, nature has had millions of years to evolve this planet into a diverse living ecosystem, where each animal and plant has fought for its place to survive. Yes, plants do fight, and fight hard, to survive. And in these fights, plants have attained such diversity it is amazing – there are some that live thousands of years (yes, thousands of years!); others feed on insects to supplement low nutrients in the soil; and still others that train animals – humans included – to protect them and to spread their seeds for future generations.

Plants training animals? Yes! As an example, you wouldn't eat a green strawberry. Why not? Because you have learned that a green strawberry is not ripe and tastes bitter; so, you leave it on the plant and wait for it to turn red. When its seeds are ready to be eaten, the strawberry plant turns the strawberry bright red to attract attention. It's saying, "Hey, look over here! Nice juicy sweet strawberry!" Once eaten, the seeds are transported to be planted away from the mother plant, expanding their territory. And by staggering the ripening of the strawberries, it guarantees that they will not all be eaten at the same time, allowing the seeds will be more widely distributed.

Did you know that only plants can make their own food from air, water and minerals, using the sun to power the manufacturing process; no animal is able to do so. It's a talent called photosynthesis, and only plants have this ability. Animals (including humans) either eat plants or eat animals that eat plants. This means that without plants, there would be no life on Earth. Plants also clean the air, absorbing carbon dioxide and releasing oxygen, creating a breathable atmosphere for the animals.

I am fascinated by how plants have learned to survive even in the most hostile of territories. When you realize that creativity is not a human invention, much can be learned by studying how plants have adapted and thrived, each in their own ecosystem. To learn many tricks and talents plants have perfected over millions of years to survive, check out one of my favorite books, Th e Private Life of Plants, by David Attenborough, and see just how vital and important plants really are, and how they have evolved to survive in almost any environment.

About the
Author

J.B. moved to Florida in her early teens and has lived there ever since, enjoying the mild weather and abundance of wildlife. She even spent several seasons raising orphan squirrels. She graduated from the University of Central Florida and has spent her working career in the legal profession. Her novels are inspired by her family and nature, as well as her need to escape from the real world once in a while.

www.facebook.com/J.B.Moonstar

Instagram
@J.B.Moonstar

Twitter
@jb_moonstar

jbmoonstar.author@gmail.com

www.jbmoonstar.com

Discover more by
JB Moonstar

Chronicles of Ituria

Russ and The Hidden Voice

Taylor and the Red Wolf Rescue

Jenna and the Legend of the White Wolf

Jenna and the Eyes of Fire

Jan and the Secret Cave

Jan and the Search for Lilya

Taylor and the Final Nine

Michelle and the Missing Manatee

Jenna and the Broken Promise

Sara and the Secret Mission

& More Adventures to Come!

The Mermaids of Crystal Cay

Kimmi and the Sea Dragon

Roselia and the Ancient Warriors

& More Adventures to Come!

Coloring Book from
Artist Jenn Kotick

Mermaids

BOOK CLUB QUESTIONS:

1. Why did Knocker think that Jenna was human when they were in the cave?

2. Why do you think Ranco was hunting in Middle Forest?

3. Are there really plants called "pitcher plants" that can hold water? If so, why do they hold water?

4. How does a Venus fl y-trap catch its prey?

5. Th e Acacia tree provides a home and food to ant colonies; what does it get in return?

6. What is the only continent on Earth where there are no plants?

7. Dandelions don't have fruit; how do their seeds get disbursed?

8. Something to think about – Ranco was thought to be hunting in Middle Forest because his North Forest was being cleared for houses. What happens to the animal residents when a forest is cleared for human use? Where can they go and how can they survive when their home is taken away from them?

Discover more at
4HorsemenPublications.com

10% off using HORSEMEN10